Mysterious Love

by Shirley Brinkerhoff

PUBLISHING
Colorado Springs, Colorado

MYSTERIOUS LOVE
Copyright © 1996 by Shirley Brinkerhoff
All rights reserved. International copyright secured.

Library of Congress Cataloging-in-Publication Data

Brinkerhoff, Shirley
    Mysterious love / Shirley Brinkerhoff
        p. cm. — (The Nikki Sheridan series ; 2)
    Summary: Involvement with a charming, but troubled new boy at school
distracts Nikki from her sadness over giving up her baby, but it is the loving
support of her grandparents and a close friend that help her resolve her feelings
of anger and guilt.
    ISBN 1-56179-485-6
    [1. Unmarried mothers—Fiction. 2. Parent and child—Fiction.
    3. Adoption —Fiction. 4. Christian life—Fiction.] I. Title. II. Series:
Brinkerhoff, Shirley. Nikki Sheridan series ; 2.
    PZ7.B780115Ci 1996
    [Fic]—dc20
                                                                96-8550
                                                                  CIP
                                                                  AC

Published by Focus on the Family Publishing,
Colorado Springs, Colorado 80995
Distributed in the U.S.A. and Canada by Word Books, Dallas, Texas.

Text from "The Glass Menagerie" by Tennessee Williams, copyright © 1945, 1973,
is reprinted by permission of Random House, Inc.

The poem "To An Adopted" from *Picture Windows*, by Carol Lynn Pearson,
Gold Leaf Press, copyright © 1996, is used by permission of the publisher.

Focus on the Family books are available at special quantity discounts when
purchased in bulk by corporations, organizations, churches, or groups. Special
imprints, messages, and excerpts can be produced to meet your needs. For more
information, write: Special Sales, Focus on the Family Publishing, 8605 Explorer
Drive, Colorado Springs, CO 80920, or call (719) 531-3400 and ask for the Special
Sales Department.

Cover Design: Candi Park
Cover Illustration: Cheri Bladholm

Printed in the United States of America

96 97 98 99 00/10 9 8 7 6 5 4 3 2 1

To my parents,
Gilbert and Dolores Hughes,
who passed on to me their love for God,
their love for books,
and their profound respect for all human life.

❧ One ❧

NIKKI STARED IN HORROR AT THE BABY playing alone on the narrow cement median in the center of the highway.

"Stop!" she screamed at the cars that streamed by, two lanes deep in either direction. "Don't you see him? *Stop!*" She waved her arms wildly and shouted till her throat burned raw with bitter exhaust fumes.

Not a single car slowed down.

The child, dressed only in a disposable diaper, toddled this way and that, his baby steps unsteady. He studied the crumbling cement beneath his feet and squatted, little-boy fashion, to pick up a pebble. Then he braced both hands flat against the ground in front of him and pushed himself up, seat first, and Nikki could make out the bright-blue ducks and elephants stamped across the plastic of his diaper.

Something at the edge of the median caught his attention, and Nikki held her breath as he wobbled closer to the speeding traffic. With all her might, she willed him to hear her thoughts.

Don't take another step. Please, please don't take another step!

A huge tanker truck, crusted with grime from the road, roared past, and the baby's sturdy little legs stumbled backward a few steps.

There's got to be a way to get to him! Nikki searched the line of cars frantically for the slightest break, for any chance to dash across the lanes. But the rushing cars formed a solid line, bumper to bumper, as far as she could see.

The baby turned and started in her direction again. He seemed fascinated by the cars. One more step and . . .

"No! Go back! Go back!" she shouted, waving him back with all her might, but it did no good. She dropped her arms and hugged them tightly around her, as though to hold in the anger exploding inside.

Who did this? she screamed silently. *What kind of monster would leave him out there, stranded, in the middle of a freeway?*

As if he sensed her presence through the watery haze of exhaust fumes, the child stopped and lifted his head. And when he did, Nikki recognized with a start the wide, blue eyes and the dark, curly hair. His soft baby chin quivered in the beginning of a cry, the same cry she'd been hearing over and over in her head for the last month.

And suddenly, Nikki knew who had left him there, and her dream dissolved in a wail of anguish.

With her mind still fuzzy from sleep, Nikki shot a glance around the bedroom to see who had cried out that way. Then she felt the pillow, crushed tight against her chest, and saw her own white-knuckled fingers clinging to the pillowcase that was damp with tears.

And she knew that all the crying in the world would never bring her baby back.

Nikki pushed herself up off the bed and staggered to her feet. The wavy glass mirror on top of the old oak dresser reflected someone she could hardly recognize. She was someone the same average height as Nikki, with the same dark, curly hair tamed back in a coral-colored band. But framed by the hair was the face of an old, old stranger, her eyes swollen small and puffy, their blue color faded from tears. Her cheeks and forehead were blotched reddish-brown, her mouth drooped, her lips were as dismal and colorless as her mood.

Nikki turned and opened the drawer of her bedside table and pulled out the pad of blue legal-sized paper and the pen lying there. She curled up on the window seat and looked out at Lake Michigan, bleak now in the gray light of winter, then tucked her freezing feet beneath her, turned back the many pages already covered with black ink and began to write.

February 26
Dear Evan,

It's a month today since you were born, and I can't help worrying about how you're doing. I know the Shiveleys are good people—I know they love you. Of all the couples I had to choose from, I really thought they'd be best.

She stopped and stared straight ahead, trying to remember. What exactly *had* it been that convinced her to choose the Shiveleys?

They were always laughing together. They were really laid-back and relaxed and all.

But now that I have to sign the final papers— Nikki glanced up at the calendar that hung beside the dresser and counted the days till March 12th *—now that the court date is just two weeks away, I'm getting more and more worried.*

When the nights get this cold, I keep wondering if Marilyn puts enough covers on you.

Nikki stopped writing and leaned her head against the windowpane, holding her breath so the cold glass wouldn't fog over. Outside, the lake was still, caught fast in swirls and hillocks of white ice that glistened in the thin, late-afternoon sunshine.

She looked down at the stack of pages she'd filled in the past month and sighed. Somehow, what had started as a letter to Evan had grown into some strange kind of journal. Writing was the only thing she had to hang on to when the dream came. She had learned she could control the pain, the agony, if she concentrated carefully on writing out every word, corralling her feelings into a paper cage.

I worry Jim will turn out to be one of those stupid dads who tosses babies way up in the air.

I wonder if he and Marilyn will answer all your questions and talk to you a lot, or if they'll be the kind of parents, like mine, who always say, "Go play. I'm too busy."

But most of all, I wonder what you'll think when you find out. About me, I mean. If you'll understand—or if you'll hate me. I wonder that all the time.

Nikki tried to keep writing, but the paper blurred in front of her eyes. In place of the rose-patterned wallpaper around her, she saw the bare, green walls of the delivery room, smelled the disinfectant and warm blood, felt the gasp of her breath as she pushed—one last immense, rending push she thought would split her body in two—and heard the sweet, rasping wail of a newborn child.

Her child.

Her memory was like a sequence of stills, the film paused at every frame.

Click. The naked, red-purple baby laid across her chest in the delivery room, squalling and flailing his tiny clenched fists at the world. Exhilaration swept over her as she stared at his perfect body, elation and love that blotted out all the terrible long hours of labor. But then hurt opened underneath the exhilaration, like a dark, yawning cavern inside her chest. She stroked the infant's dark, wet hair and he quieted, as if by magic. *He's a part of me. But he'll never be mine.*

Click. The baby's wide, staring blue eyes that peered, struggling to focus, from under the edge of the knitted blue cap. Eventually, they found Nikki's face and locked on to it. She rubbed her chin gently over his velvety cheek and breathed in the sweet fragrance of his skin.

Click. Jim and Marilyn Shiveley, the family she had chosen to raise her son, trying unsuccessfully to hold in their excitement and their smiles in the face of her grief. Their arms reached eagerly to hold the baby, pull him into their small circle—the circle that excluded her.

Click. The papers she signed, sitting propped up against pillows in the hospital bed.

"It's an open adoption," the nurse tried to encourage her. "You'll get letters and pictures, and you'll get to see him often. It's so much better this way."

Better.

Better?

Downstairs, the grandfather clock chimed six times—six deep, hollow *bongs* that echoed through the house. Nikki looked up, startled. She had meant to take only a short nap when she laid down at 4:00, and now she'd barely be ready by the time Chad came to pick her up.

Why do I even want to go? her reflection in the window glass against the growing evening darkness seemed to ask.

Because, she told the reflection, *the only thing you can do is get out of here and keep busy—so busy you won't think—and Chad is your best bet for tonight.*

Nikki jerked the cord, and the satin drapes snapped shut across the window. She slipped the blue tablet and pen carefully back in the drawer of her bedside table.

"*It's time to forget what's past,*" she parroted, "*to put it all behind you and get on with life.*" Those were the words the social worker kept saying to her in the hospital, as Nikki sat in the wheelchair, ready to be wheeled to the exit doors to go home.

"*Get on with life.*" Nikki could still see the social worker's acne-scarred face, earnest with her serious mission of handing out advice. The lenses of her thick glasses had flashed and glinted in the flat fluorescent light of the hospital hall, and Nikki squirmed with embarrassment because the young, black orderly who brought the wheelchair could hear every word she said. But the social worker was oblivious. "*Thousands of young women go through this every year, and they go on to live happy, successful lives. So just—*"

I know, I know, already! Just put it all behind me and get on with life, Nikki had thought. *Which might be a possibility, if I can ever get out of here.*

Now, a month later, she glanced at her watch, gathered her white terrycloth robe around her, and hurried down the hall to the shower.

Get on with life. Get on with life.

The words played over and over in her head like the melody from some popular song stuck there, until the air in the bathroom water pipes stuttered a loud bass rumble and the thin, rusty-looking spray cleared to a hot, steady stream. She stepped under the steaming water and leaned her head far forward so it could wet all of her hair, and maybe even wash away the thoughts.

Back in her bedroom, Nikki switched on the dryer and plied her thick tangle of hair with an oversized, round brush, trying to straighten out at least some of the curl. Thankful the long, hot shower had erased the puffy, blotchy patches crying always left on her face, she smoothed on pale-beige foundation that matched her skin and tried to decide what to wear. She searched the dresser drawers, inspecting stretch pants and tunics, jeans and sweaters— and she groaned.

The blue sweater looked best, but the only thing she could wear it with was jeans, and jeans were a definite problem. Nikki eyed them with distaste. She was back to her prepregnancy weight, but somehow that weight seemed to be spread around a lot differently. Anything that snapped, buttoned, or zipped at the waist was now a major challenge.

She sighed. It wouldn't make any difference for tonight, but she was absolutely determined to be faithful about exercising every day.

She lowered herself to the floor and started her 45 sit-ups. With one eye on the clock, she forced herself up and down, up and down, until she reached her goal.

Then she flipped over to her stomach on the scratchy old carpet, facing its faded roses, and pushed herself up on her hands and knees for the "cat." She arched her back, pulled her stomach muscles taut till they hurt, then held them that way while she counted slowly to 10. "Listen," the nurse at the hospital had told her, "you do 10 of these a day and that stomach'll be flatter than a board in no time."

Right, Nikki thought as she sucked in her muscles and breath for another repetition. *And just exactly how long is "no time"?*

When she ran downstairs, still holding her stomach in so the waistband of her jeans didn't pinch so hard, the smell of roast and potatoes filled the air.

"Grandpa? You need some help with dinner? I thought I'd be late, but I still have a few minutes till Chad gets here."

Her grandfather poured a half cup of golden olive oil into a glass cruet he held at eye level, checking the measurement lines as carefully as though it were one of his lab beakers. "No, I think dinner's under control, honey."

He turned and glanced at her, then quickly looked away as he corked the cruet and shook it. She couldn't help noticing how much deeper the lines in his forehead and the creases around his mouth were this winter, and she wondered how much of that was her doing.

Between Nikki's pregnancy, with all the trouble it had caused in the family, and Gram's stroke, Grandpa had had to put aside almost all his research and writing for the past seven months, spending endless hours cooking and helping his wife with her therapy.

Gram smiled up at Nikki from her seat at the kitchen table, and Gallie, the Nobles's golden retriever, sat quietly with his head in her lap, thumping the floor gently with his feathery tail to let Nikki know he acknowledged her, too.

At least Gram can smile again, Nikki thought. The stroke had left one side of her face slack and useless for several months, but now, with intense therapy and exercise, the weakness was hardly noticeable. She could walk again, too, though the entire left side of her body was still weaker than the right, a fact that routinely drove

Nikki's once-active grandmother to exasperation.

Even her ability to talk was coming back, little by little, thanks to hours of speech therapy. But she still remained silent much of the time, and Nikki was sure that was because it required such intense concentration for Gram to make her tongue form words.

Months ago, Nikki's Aunt Marta, the younger of Gram's two daughters and a musicologist, had discovered that her mother could sing words she couldn't say. "A stroke can damage the speech control center of the brain and leave the area that controls music entirely untouched," she had explained.

So whenever Marta could get home for a visit, she worked with her mother for hours, singing all the old hymns and songs from musicals she knew Gram loved. But her job as assistant music professor at Indiana State, plus all the music seminars and conferences she did around the country, left little time for her to get back to the blue clapboard house in Rosendale, Michigan. That meant it fell to Nikki to spend an hour or so each day singing and practicing sentences with Gram.

During the long months of Nikki's pregnancy, Gram's therapy had helped pass the time. But now that the baby was born, Nikki found to her shame that she was growing more and more impatient with her grandmother's inch-by-inch progress.

She sat down in the chair across from Gram and buttered a slice of bread, then cut it in two and set it neatly on her grandmother's plate. "There you go, Gram. Saves you some time for more important things, like that roast I smell."

"It's a beauty, too," Grandpa put in. "Sure you won't have a piece before you go?"

"Thanks, Grandpa, but we're getting something to eat on the way to play practice, remember?"

Gram smiled again and spoke slowly. "He'll never know."

"What?" Nikki said, frowning as she tried to decipher her grandmother's meaning. Then she caught on. "Oh! You mean Chad'll never know if I eat here and there, too?"

Gram dipped her head in acknowledgment and grinned.

Nikki burst out laughing. "Right, Gram! The idea these days is to eat *less*, not more. I can hardly get my jeans buttoned."

"He's good," Gram said, inclining her head slightly toward her husband.

Nikki considered her meaning again, then laughed. "Who? Grandpa? Well—" she lowered her voice to a stage whisper, pretending her grandfather couldn't hear "—I think he's turned into a pretty great cook since last summer, too, but I wouldn't want to say so in front of him. It could give him a big head, you know?"

"Talk about teaching an old dog new tricks," Grandpa said as he carefully set the hot roast and potatoes on the table in front of them, then untied Gram's blue-flowered apron from around his waist. But Nikki noticed his usual smile was missing, along with the absentminded, tuneless whistling through his teeth that usually accompanied his kitchen work and had been known to drive even Gram to plead, *"Roger! Please!"*

"Never knew I had it in me to be a master chef, but this isn't so different from cutting up specimens in the biology lab all those years," he said as he inched the chair in behind him, then began to cut the meat on Gram's plate into bite-sized pieces.

"By the way, Nikki," he began, and Nikki got the distinct impression that he was working hard to sound casual, "did you see the letter I left on the dining room table for you?"

"No. I was so tired when I came in from school that I went right upstairs for a nap." She pushed back her chair, and the wooden legs scraped against the white kitchen linoleum. "Who's it from?"

Grandpa drew his knife precisely through the last piece of

meat, then looked up to meet her eyes for the first time since she'd entered the kitchen. "It's from your mother."

Nikki's lips drew together in a thin, tight line, and she stopped, halfway out of her chair.

"Nikki," Grandpa said hesitantly, and Nikki could see the strain on his face.

She stood up and started for the dining room door. "Okay, okay. I'll go get it."

She turned and made her way to the dining room, snatched the envelope off the table, and stared at the sharp-edged black ink curved gracefully into the letters of her name. Then she turned and pounded up the stairs to her room, jerked open the bottom dresser drawer, and pulled back the pile of jeans shorts and brightly colored T-shirts left from summer.

She thrust the letter into the farthest corner of the drawer, pushed the clothes down over it, and stood back up, kicking the drawer shut with her foot. Her fingers clenched the edges of the dresser top, and her breath came fast and hard, but not from sprinting up the stairs. She stared again at her own reflection in the mirror.

This time, her eyes were no longer swollen from tears. They were narrowed and intensely blue, and her cheeks and lips were flushed red with anger. She was shocked at how much she looked like David Sheridan, her father, with his flashing eyes and curly hair—and how little like her mother, with her perfectly permed brown hair, her light skin, and green eyes. Rachel was always cool and sleekly calm, whether on stage singing opera or—Nikki winced at the memory—riding along in the car as she and Nikki's father drove their only daughter to the clinic for an abortion. An abortion *they* had planned and scheduled, with no input from Nikki.

Why can't she just leave me alone? Nikki cried at the reflection. *They're the ones who walked out on me, her and Dad. They're the ones who said, "Don't bother coming home pregnant."*

And it had all worked out for them, too. Nikki's father, who had feared that having a pregnant, unmarried daughter would bring his career plans to a screeching halt, got his appointment as judge of family court back home in Millbrook, Ohio. Her mother, basking in the reflected light of her newly-important spouse, was now an assistant professor at the junior college instead of a part-time instructor. And she was performing more than ever.

All that stuff they dreamed about, Nikki thought, *they got it all. And I got to stay here with Gram and Grandpa and have the baby—and give him up, to people I hardly know.*

She kicked the bottom drawer shut even tighter for good measure and wished she had the nerve to tear her mother's letter to shreds and flush it down the toilet. Or toss it into one of Grandpa's roaring fireplace blazes.

She's probably still telling me to stand up straight and quit peeling my fingernails. Or— Nikki thought of her mother's all-time favorite admonition *—to start taking control of my life.*

"Keep your letter, Mother," she hissed at the mirror through clenched teeth. "And keep your neat little life and your neat little career. I won't ever get in your way again."

Downstairs, Gram and Grandpa watched her quietly as Nikki walked with forced nonchalance back into the kitchen, hoping the redness had faded from her cheeks.

"Well?" Grandpa asked, his fork in midair, with a chunk of roast impaled on the tines.

"Well what?"

"Did you read it?"

Nikki looked at them both, and her dark eyebrows drew closer together.

"Nikki," Grandpa began again, "you know—"

"Listen," she broke in. "I don't mean to be rude, Grandpa, but there's absolutely no way I'm reading that letter. She walked out on me, remember?"

A horn honked in the driveway outside the kitchen door, and Nikki grabbed her jacket from the coat tree. She turned to face her grandparents with one hand on the doorknob. "As far as I'm concerned, I never want to see either of my parents or speak to them again as long as I live!"

❧ *Two* ❧

"SO, YOU UP FOR A LITTLE change in plans?" Chad slid his right arm across the back of Nikki's seat and around her shoulders, steering the LeSabre with two fingers of his left hand.

"What kind of change?" Nikki asked, frowning.

Chad gave a long, low whistle under his breath and shook his head. "I never can figure it out."

"Figure what out? What are you talking about?"

"Whether I like it better when those big blue eyes of yours are smiling at me or when you're watching me like I'm about to haul you off to some dark corner and—" he switched to a deep bass, theatrical voice "—*ha-hah! Have my way with you!*"

He put both hands back on the steering wheel as he switched to a Humphrey Bogart voice. "I just know I like it, sweetheart. I like it." Then he drummed an intricate syncopated rhythm against the black vinyl, letting the car steer itself for a moment.

Nikki laughed in spite of herself. She could never help laughing at Chad. "Fine. So you like it. We've established that. But I still don't know what change in plans you're talking about. I like to have at least a vague idea where I'm going, if you wouldn't mind."

"You know, my dear—" Chad's voice took on the clipped, singsong tone of W. C. Fields "—back in my day, the little woman went along with the man, just went along. You know what I mean? But you, Nikki, you are a suspicious woman, a *modern* woman, but I'll humor you, ummm-hmmm. I'll humor you because—" he waggled his eyebrows at her and his glance slid down to her waist and back up again in exaggerated fashion "—you're beautiful, my little chickadee. Absolutely mah-velous."

Nikki punched him lightly on the arm. "Come on, Chad. Get serious. What're we doing?"

"Reach in my jacket pocket. See what you find."

Nikki stuck her hand in the pocket of his soft, brown leather jacket, pulled out two tickets, and held them close to the dim light of the dashboard.

"Black Tail Spin! You're kidding!" Then she frowned. "Where'd you get these tickets? This concert's been sold out for a month."

He glanced at her sideways, waggled his eyebrows again, and smirked. "That's for me to know, and you never, ever to find out. I can't give away all my secrets, you know."

"Really, Chad, where'd you get them?"

"Really, Nikki," he mocked her seriousness, "I'll never tell."

"But what about play practice tonight? You can't just not show. Mr. Keaton'll have a major fit."

Chad gave a short laugh and drummed another quick rhythm on the steering wheel.

"Well?" she insisted.

He held his right hand to the side of his head, his thumb extended like an earpiece, his little finger in front of his mouth. When he spoke, his voice sounded uncannily like someone's father. "'Hello, Dick Keaton there? Chad's had a little accident with my LeSabre. Nothing terribly serious, you understand, but they want him in the hospital overnight for observation. They think there may be a slight concussion. Sorry he has to miss practice tonight, but I can't possibly let him put himself in danger. What's that? Oh, certainly, I'll be sure to tell him. He'll appreciate that.'" Chad folded his hand, hung up with a click of his tongue against the roof of his mouth, then grinned at Nikki again.

"You didn't!" she said.

"You don't know me very well yet, do you, Nicole?"

You're right, Nikki thought. *I don't.*

It had been only two weeks since she first caught sight of Chad in the hall at school. She'd been hurrying, trying to catch up with Keesha Riley before English. Chad was shaking the principal's hand and introducing himself, with a perfectly straight face.

"That's right, sir," she'd heard him say as she walked past. "The name is Seymour Davies, and I'll *see more* of you later." He emphasized the two words just enough to suggest insolence.

Nikki's eyes had opened wide, waiting for the principal's response, but the older man only stood there, speechless, as his newest student turned and followed Nikki down the hall.

She tried to act as if she was unaware of him walking just behind her, but her shoulders were shaking with laughter. Nobody at Howellsville paid much attention to Mr. Peabody, the high school principal, but nobody spoke to him that way either.

Until now.

Nikki kept walking. From behind her came the long, low whistle that she would soon know so well.

"So this is what they mean by the Michigan Model, hmm? And here all this time I thought they were talking about an educational concept." The voice aped Humphrey Bogart, low and growly. "So give us a name, sweetheart, give us a name." When she still didn't turn around, the voice switched to an exaggerated Southern drawl as he followed her through the doorway to English class. "Well, shoot, Buford, at least turn around and let us have a look."

Nikki slid into her seat across the aisle from Keesha, trying hard to hold in the laughter and ignore him. But her curiosity won.

She glanced up at his blue-striped oxford shirt, open at the neck, at the slender maroon tie knotted with exactly the right amount of slack, and all the other guys in the room suddenly looked awkward and immature, shuffling to their seats in baggy shirts and uniformly faded jeans.

Chad's thick blond hair fell sideways across his nearly-black brows and eyes. The contrast was as surprising as his outrageous behavior.

"Who are you, anyway?" she finally burst out. "Is your first name really *Seymour?*"

"Are you kidding? I don't even have a first name, just a string of last names you wouldn't believe—Chadwick Seymour Severenson Davies . . . the Third." He grabbed a pencil from behind his ear and the pen out of Nikki's hand and drummed an intricate rhythm on the top of her desk. "But *you* can call me Chad. Or—" his dark eyebrows rose suggestively, and he leaned so close she could smell the clean scent of soap on his skin and see tiny flecks of yellow in his dark eyes "—just about anything else you'd like."

Mr. Keaton strutted into the classroom then, his toes turned inward in the pigeon-toed walk that produced a slight waddle and always made students whisper unfortunate comparisons to certain ducks in the village park. Chad swung around to face the front of the room.

Bryce Putnam, one of the school's football greats and a senior repeating junior English in one last desperate attempt to graduate, sauntered in, as always, just behind Mr. Keaton. He pushed his way down the row between the desks where Nikki and Keesha sat.

"Hey, Nik!" Keesha hissed after he passed. "You forgot to bow!"

Keesha was the only other student at Howellsville High School who was pregnant this year, so she and Nikki, lumped together by the rest of the school as two of a kind, had gravitated toward one another.

"Word's out that if our famous quarterback doesn't do good on the research paper, he doesn't have a chance of passing this course," Keesha went on.

But Nikki barely heard her. Instead, she stared at the back of Chad's head, at the blond hair that curled down over his blue collar, and wondered how he could be so much like all those loudmouthed guys she could never stomach, and yet so different. *He's just another showoff*, she thought, trying to dismiss him in her mind, but she couldn't. Other guys who did things like that might come across as jerks, but there was something different about Chad. Not to mention his looks, which, Nikki noticed as she scanned the room, had already caught the attention of half the class—the female half.

And she had to admit, it felt wonderful to laugh again. It was her first week back to classes after the baby was born, and she hadn't had anything to smile about in weeks. Now, in just five minutes, this Chadwick Seymour Severenson Davies, the *Third*, had made her laugh so hard she couldn't stop.

Mr. Keaton spent the first five minutes of class reminding everyone that the papers due in two weeks counted 50 percent of their grades, and that absolutely no late papers would be accepted.

"Yawn, yawn," Keesha said from across the aisle. "Haven't we heard all this before?"

Then Mr. Keaton introduced Chad and asked where he'd

come from. Chad stood with exaggerated politeness and told the class he was from New York City. "I moved here to Michigan with my father. He . . . changed jobs."

Mr. Keaton eyed him carefully as he spoke, then asked Chad if he'd ever had any experience in drama.

Keesha moaned. "Here we go again," she said from behind her hand. "The only thing old Keaton ever thinks about is his next play. All he did while you were gone was try and recruit people to be in it!" She slid down in her seat and folded her arms across her bulging stomach.

Keesha never minced words, and she was even more vocal than most about Mr. Keaton's obvious preference for directing drama over teaching his English classes.

She tossed her headful of beaded braids back over her shoulders and pursed her lips as she stared up at Chad's wide shoulders and blond hair. "But this time, I think he uncovered a major babe. Too bad he's the wrong color," she laughed, then her lips turned down as her black hands patted her protruding abdomen. "Not that I'm attracting many guys of *any* color, these days."

"Keesha, please!" Mr. Keaton demanded, and Keesha grinned and squeezed two fingers together over her mouth to show that her lips were sealed.

Chad answered Mr. Keaton's question smoothly—a little too smoothly, Nikki thought. "Well, I've done some. I was in *Romeo and Juliet* last year, and the year before that I was in *Exit the Body*." Nikki could see Mr. Keaton's eyes light up. "Twentieth century American plays are my special interest. Sir."

"Get out of here!" Keesha laughed so hard her shoulders shook. "Look at Keaton, Nik. He doesn't even know this guy's putting him on. If we're lucky, he may get so excited he'll cancel class and try to hold a rehearsal right here."

"Well," Mr. Keaton said, rubbing his hands together with a dry, papery sound, "I'll certainly look forward to talking to you about this after class."

"Absolutely. I will, too. Sir."

As Mr. Keaton bent to open his text to the section of *Beowulf* assigned for the day, Chad turned toward the classroom, pointed back over his shoulder toward the teacher with a hitchhiker's thumb, and rolled his eyes toward the acoustic-tile ceiling, then sat down quickly. The entire class burst out laughing, and Mr. Keaton looked up with a puzzled frown.

"Clueless," Keesha groaned and shook her head. "The man is absolutely clueless."

Now, back in the car, Chad slid his right arm around Nikki's shoulders again, and she could smell the soft leather of his jacket sleeve. "You still haven't given me an answer."

"What? Oh, about the concert, you mean? Can we get something to eat first?"

Chad laughed and ran his right hand through Nikki's hair as he drove. "Naturally. Think I'd let you starve? But you'll have to eat fast."

When they opened the doors to the Columbia City Arena, the music—which had been a thin, distant pulse in the street—hit them full in the face like a wave. Nikki stopped dead for a second in the doorway, waiting for her ears to adjust. The floor beneath her feet shook in time to the bass guitar, and all around her, closely-packed bodies moved in rhythm to the shaking.

"C'mon, I wanna get up close," Chad yelled above the noise.

He urged her forward, but no matter how she pushed, she couldn't make enough headway. Chad stepped in front of her, pulled her arms tight around his waist, and started to work his way through the crowd.

Finally, halfway to the front of the arena, they hit a solid wall of bodies. "Guess this is as far as we go," he shouted at her.

Nikki started to reclaim her arms, but he held them in place around his waist. The crowd was packed so tightly against her and Chad that it was impossible for her to move away.

At first the wall of people around them only swayed in rhythm, then a ripple of movement began near the stage. The ripple spread and grew, and soon the front half of the arena, packed with hundreds of bodies, started to move back and forth together, arms high above their heads, hands clapping in unison to the beat.

It was like watching a single animal, driven by the tempo of the music. Back. Forward. Back. Forward. When the song finally ended, the bass guitarist laughed and held a bottle high, took a long drink, then thundered into a wild sequence of scales that set the crowd moving frenetically again, most of them simply dancing in place. The music went on and on, through more songs than Nikki could count, and her back muscles, still strained from all those sit-ups, began to ache.

Then people in front scrambled onto the stage and began crowd surfing from its edge. Caught up in the rhythm pounding from the speakers, Nikki watched in fascination. Some, mostly guys, stood with arms raised high, then hurled themselves off the stage backward. The girls seemed more cautious at first, but the band urged the divers on, their playing growing more and more frenzied as the crowd warmed up.

Chad tried again and again to push his way through to the

stage, but the press of bodies held him fast. Finally, he leaned his head back toward her so she could just make out his voice over the sound that surged around them. "Next time," he yelled, nodding toward the front of the crowd, "we get here early, and I'm gonna be up there!"

"Isn't it kind of dangerous?" Nikki yelled back.

Chad's lips closed into a thin, mocking line. "So next time I'll take you to see Lawrence Welk, okay?"

Then, abruptly, the noise around them died and the motion of the crowd slid to a standstill. Nikki looked around, confused at the sudden silence ringing in her ears.

Moving to the front of the stage were five burly security guards, motioning at the crowd surfers to stop. Nikki turned her head. More guards took up their positions around the perimeter of the stage.

"Muscle-bound freaks," Chad said, just loud enough to be heard by the people close to him. "Why don't you mind your own business!"

Other voices echoed his thoughts, only in stronger words. But under the gaze of the guards, who stood with their arms folded across their chests and their faces impassive, the concert seemed to fizzle. The band's attempt to reignite the crowd petered out after two more intense, ear-splitting numbers, and though the music continued, most of the fans on the floor now seemed more interested in the bottles being passed furtively from hand to hand and the smell of marijuana, which hung sweet and heavy in the air.

When the concert finally ended and Chad and Nikki thronged with everyone else through the doors of the arena, the icy winter darkness felt almost unbearably bleak and still. The overwhelming noise of the band, the colors and lights, and the heat and crush of thousands of bodies had achieved what Nikki had been unable to do for the past month—they had deadened all the painful memories.

But now, as they slid into the front seat of the LeSabre and headed across the frozen landscape toward Rosendale, Nikki was glad for Chad's warm arm around her shoulders, for his crazy jokes and voices. Because out here in the darkness, all the memories—of Evan, of his birth a month ago tonight—were still waiting. They clamored at her through the dark windows of the car, threatening to overwhelm her.

"Nikki. Nikki!" Chad's arm tightened around her shoulders. "You're dreaming again. How about coming back to me?"

"Sorry," she said. "I was just thinking."

"About what?"

She could never discuss Evan with Chad. He knew she'd placed her baby for adoption, but she'd made it clear the subject was off-limits. "Nothing much. Never mind."

"Okay, have it your way. You want to play mysterious, that's fine with me. So what'd you think of the concert?"

Nikki turned to face him, unable to fight off the depression that was beginning to swallow her once again. "It was okay, I guess."

"Whoa. Talk about enthusiasm!" Chad winced and put a hand over his heart. "Don't sugarcoat it on my behalf! I practically had to kill for those tickets, but hey, who cares about that, right?"

Chad switched on the radio and sampled several stations. He paused at a talk show that caught his interest, and Nikki found herself listening as a man's voice spoke.

"I just don't think I can ever get over this," the voice came through the car's speakers. "It's been a year and I still can't forget—"

A woman's voice, crisp and decisive, cut in. "And you shouldn't."

"I shouldn't?" the man responded in surprise. "But I thought—"

"Look, John, your wife betrayed you. As a psychologist, I'm

telling you this is probably the worst single thing one person can do to another, and she did it to you. You can't forget a thing like that."

The man's voice came back, thin and high. "But how do I live with the pain?"

"Hey, what do you want me to say, John? If there was some quick fix for this kind of pain, don't you think I'd give it to you? Hmmm?"

"Well . . . my wife says I should forgive her."

The psychologist laughed. "John, you're not listening to me. I just told you, there's no such thing as a quick fix, remember? That's all she wants. Maybe what you need to do is show her how it feels to be betrayed this way. Have you thought about that?"

Nikki listened, uneasy at the advice the talk show host was giving, but Chad laughed out loud.

"Just give it right back to her!" he agreed, as he switched back to a music channel. "I wish somebody'd tell my old man that."

"Why?" Nikki asked, her own thoughts swallowed by Chad's sudden change of mood.

He turned and looked at her, startled, and Nikki knew she'd caught him off guard. Then his mouth settled into a kind of sneer.

"I'll spare you all the gory details, okay, Nikki? Let's just say that my mom decided about a year ago that some accountant she worked with looked a lot better to her than my dad, if you know what I mean. They live out in the Rockies now, some yuppie ski town where that kind of thing's just fine."

"You mean, she just left?"

"You catch on fast, Nikki. Anybody ever tell you that before?"

"What about the rest of your family?"

"Tell me, ma'am," he said, trying for a lighter note, "do you work for 'Inside Edition'? Or is it 'Hard Copy'? And will this be the lead story, or will it get stuck in the last 47 seconds of the program?" He dropped the bantering tone. "As far as the rest of my family goes, you're looking at it, babe. I'm the last kid still at home, and I just stay out of the house as much as I can."

"What about your dad?"

Chad braked at a red light, felt around under the front seat, and pulled out an empty whiskey bottle. "See this?"

Nikki nodded.

"I found this one just before I picked you up. It rolled out from under the seat and hit my foot. If you look close, you can pretty much see a path on the carpet from all the other ones that've rolled out, too. Then there's the ones that show up in the bottom of the laundry basket, or out in the garbage can, wrapped up in bags or newspaper. He thinks he's *hiding* them, if you can believe that. His mind's been pretty screwed up since Mom left."

He was silent for a moment, then continued. "You know that 'job change' I said my dad made? Well, let's just say it wasn't his idea. He was vice president of my grandfather's company for 15 years, but my grandfather—that'd be Chadwick Seymour Severenson Davies the *First*, in case you're getting confused here— doesn't put up with some drunk messing up the company books, even if it's because the guy's wife ran off. Even if it's his own son. Anyway, that's all you ever need to know about my dad."

Outside, snow started to fall around the car—huge, lacy flakes that settled silently on the hood and the windshield and curtained the yellow pools of light beneath the street lamps.

Nikki thought about her own parents . . . about the anger on her father's face when he'd found out his plans for her to have an abortion had not succeeded, the day he turned and walked out of her life . . . about the mingled confusion and sorrow on her mother's face as she turned to follow him . . . about her own feelings at being left behind by both of them. *Why would Mother write to me now? After all these months?*

"Sorry I asked, Chad," she said quietly.

"Hey, inquiring minds want to know, right?" He gave a short, harsh laugh. "Listen, you know that old business about kids being seen and not heard? Well, *my* philosophy is that *parents* shouldn't be seen, shouldn't be heard, and should be thought of as little as possible."

He drummed out the rhythm of one of the songs the band had played at the concert and started singing the words. When Nikki remained silent, he reached out and pulled her closer. "Sing with me, babe. C'mon. *C'mon!*"

∞ Three ∞

"NIKKI? IS THAT YOU?" Grandpa's soft voice called as she let herself in the house and turned toward the strip of light showing under the study door.

"How come you're up so late?" Nikki asked as she pushed open the door and surveyed her grandfather's desk, covered with open biology texts stacked two and three deep and journals pulled from the wall of books behind his ancient wooden swivel chair. "Hey, you're working on another article, aren't you?"

In the soft light of the green-shaded desk lamp, the deep creases around his mouth were eased. His hair, which had been salt-and-pepper gray before Gram's stroke, was now completely white, but it framed the same warm smile, the same bright blue eyes that had never, in all of Nikki's 17 years, looked at her with anything but love.

Grandpa took off his silver-rimmed glasses and rubbed at the red spots they left on either side of his nose. "The editor at *Scientific Journal* called this morning and asked if I'd consider starting again, and I told him I'd take a shot at it, now that your Gram's doing so much better."

He settled his glasses back in place, then grinned up at Nikki. "Actually, I feel like a kid back on the playground. Oh, and Nikki—" He searched through the books and journals in front of him until he found a slip of paper underneath one of them and held it out to her. There were two phone numbers scrawled on it in pencil. "Jeff Allen called and wants you to call him back. And Keesha—isn't she the one you always talk about who's due to have her baby soon?"

Nikki nodded.

"Well, she called to see why you and Chad weren't at play practice tonight." He looked at her questioningly.

"We decided to go into Columbia instead. Chad got some tickets to the Black Tail Spin concert at the last minute."

Grandpa's eyebrows raised. "Oh, really? I hear things get pretty rough at some of those concerts."

Nikki shrugged. Telling him about the crowd surfing and the drinking was out of the question. "It was fine, Grandpa. Really."

Still he watched her.

"Don't worry about it, okay?" she said, more sharply than she intended.

Nikki took the paper from her grandfather and turned to go, but his voice stopped her.

"Can you sit and talk for a minute, honey?"

Something in his voice made her reluctant to agree, but she couldn't very well just walk away. She sat down hesitantly on the edge of the soft leather couch across from his desk. "I guess so."

There was a short *beep* from the computer as he closed down his file, then switched off the power.

"I didn't want to say much about this around your grandma," he said. "You know how bad any kind of family stress is for her right now."

Family stress? Nikki slouched back against the brown cushions. *That pretty much gives away what we're talking about here, right from the top.*

He went on, choosing his words carefully. "Nikki, I know that what your parents did to you last summer was devastating."

Nikki folded her arms across her chest and stared at the toes of her brown suede shoes.

"I think your attitude was great through the whole pregnancy. You just did what had to be done. Your grandma and I were very proud of you." He picked up his pen and tapped the point of it lightly against his desk. "Now, though, several things have happened that make me think you're really struggling with anger about it."

"Why *shouldn't* I be angry?" Nikki broke in. "Wouldn't you be? Wouldn't *anybody* in their right mind? Anyway, it doesn't matter anymore. They got what they wanted—me out of their lives! And they're out of mine. Completely. *Totally.*"

"Well, that's not exactly true, Nikki. It's a funny thing, but sometimes when you're so angry at someone, you end up carrying them around in your mind all the time. Sometimes it's easier in the long run to, well—" he hesitated, then put both palms up "—to forgive."

Nikki jumped to her feet, her cheeks burning, and stood in front of his desk. "*Forgive?* You talk like it's as easy as pulling a rabbit out of a hat. What am I supposed to do? Just smile and pretend that what they did was all right?"

"Not at all. You're confusing 'forgiving' and 'excusing.' I'm not talking about pretending your parents had some excuse to behave as they did. I'm talking about recognizing that what they did was wrong, then choosing to forgive it."

He watched her shake her head back and forth and added, "Nikki, all I can tell you is that, as you get older, you never regret the times you forgave, the times you tried to put relationships back together—you only regret the times you *didn't*. I think the Lord had a very good reason for putting those words about 'forgive us our sins as we forgive those who sin against us' into the prayer He taught His disciples, because the two go hand in hand. Being forgiven and forgiving. Remember when Carole and I taught you that prayer? When you were about this high?" He held his hand even with the edge of the desk and smiled at her, but Nikki didn't smile back.

She could feel the anger rising in her throat, and she knew she should stop, but the words seemed to tumble out on their own. "What would you know about having to forgive people, anyway? How could you *possibly* know, you and Gram? Sure, this last year's been rotten, with Gram's stroke and me getting pregnant and all, but up until then, your life was great. What do you know about forgiving people who treat you like dirt?"

Grandpa's lips closed in a thin, tight smile for a minute, and Nikki stood there hating herself for speaking to him that way. Finally, he answered.

"You know one of the most interesting things about young people, Nikki? Their own lifetime is all they can ever imagine. You've been around for 17 years now, but Carole and I were married for nearly a quarter of a century before you were even born. And we knew each other long before that." One side of his mouth turned up just a little. "There may be a few things you don't know about this family. Just a few."

"I don't want to talk about this family anymore."

She could hear Chad's voice, *"Parents shouldn't be seen, shouldn't be heard, and should be thought of as little as possible."*

"And if you don't mind," she added, "I'm going up to bed now."

Grandpa sighed and nodded. "If that's what you want. Just remember, I'm here if you want to talk more. Oh, and Nikki?" She turned back to face him, her hand on the study door. "Don't forget about the time difference between here and Chicago. Jeff said to call him up until midnight, his time."

Nikki glanced at her watch. It was quarter to one, so she still had 15 minutes. She turned and made her way up the stairs.

Gram needed all the sleep she could get since the stroke, so Nikki tiptoed past her grandmother's bedroom door, avoiding the floorboards that squeaked. She lifted the phone from the hall table and carried it to her bedroom, trailing the long cord behind her, then shut the door silently.

In the shaded light of the small, white bedside lamp, she curled up on the flowered comforter and started to punch Jeff's number into the phone. But as her fingers hovered over the last four digits, she stopped. Just thinking about Jeff opened up a flood of memories from last summer.

Suddenly, she was back on the green-forested dune above Lake Michigan, where Jeff had listened, with his arms around her, while she sobbed out the whole story about T.J. and how she got pregnant.

She could remember exactly how he'd looked, the day after Gram's stroke, standing in the elevator doorway at the hospital, his battered fishing hat jammed back off his forehead.

"Come see the fireworks with me, Nik," he'd said, nodding his head at the dreary hospital hallway. "You need a break from all this."

And she could see him as he looked just a month ago, at the hospital again. Only this time *she* had been the patient. He had bent over her bed, his face nearly hidden by the huge bouquet of flowers he held out to her.

She'd checked her watch, though she knew all too well it was 2:00 A.M., as she'd been marking every quarter hour, lying there staring into the darkness, ever since the nurse switched off the light at 11:00.

"I came as soon as I could, Nik." Jeff laid the flowers on the tray table beside the bed and bent his hands around the metal railing. In the light from the open door, she could make out his long, dark eyelashes. "We had an away game, and when I got home, Mom said you, uh, you signed the preliminary papers today. I thought you might need some cheering up."

"You drove three hours to bring me flowers?" Her voice wavered just a bit on the last word.

Somehow, then, both his hands left the metal bedrail and wrapped themselves around hers, the warmth of his fingers spreading to her own. The darkness of the hospital room seemed to shrink. "Nik? I've been praying for you this whole time."

Nikki smiled a half-smile, remembering the look on Jeff's face, his grin, the waist-high wave he'd given her when the nurse discovered him and ushered him out the door with a stern warning about sneaking into people's hospital rooms in the middle of the night.

It seems like it all happened to someone else, in some other lifetime.

She started to punch in the last four digits of his phone number, then stopped and stared around the bedroom, undecided.

And maybe I should just leave it that way.

After a minute, she set the phone on the bedside table and started to pull her blue sweater over her head. The sweet smell of Chad's cologne lingered in the wool, and she took a deep breath, thinking back over the evening.

Chad was just about the only person who could make her laugh these days. She pretended a lot around Gram and Grandpa, laughing and joking and trying to act as though everything was back to normal. But Chad made her laugh for real with those crazy accents, the nutty things he did.

She pulled her arms out of the sleeves and dropped the sweater on the bed. On the other hand, she could never see Chad driving three hours to bring someone flowers. But where Jeff brought back memories just by being around, Chad made her stop thinking about . . . things. At least for a while.

Nikki drew a fuzzy flannel nightshirt down over her shoulders and listened to the howl of the wind that was picking up off the lake. She pictured Evan in his crib at the Shiveleys, breathing quietly in the glow of the dark room.

What if Marilyn forgets to check him before she goes to sleep and he doesn't have enough covers? She felt again the warm velvet of his dusky cheeks, the petal softness of his tiny feet and fingers. That day in the hospital—the one day she'd had with him—she stroked those hands and feet in wonder, thinking that there had never before been anything so soft in the whole wide world.

She shoved back the comforter and woolen blankets, crawled into bed, and opened the drawer of the bedside table. She picked up her pen and pad of paper, then carefully drew out an envelope that lay beneath them. From it, she pulled a thin paper with curled-up edges.

She smoothed the creases open on the bed in front of her, then stared at the black-and-white ultrasound picture for a long moment. Then she continued the letter she'd started earlier that day.

I remember how you looked just a month ago tonight, when they first brought you into my room. You were all wrapped up in receiving blankets and you smelled sweet, like baby lotion. Your eyes were wide open and dark blue and you kept looking around at everything like you were totally fascinated. Especially the lights.

I guess the reason I can't forget that night is because it was such a surprise. I knew I had to take care of you, Evan, from the first day I saw you on the ultrasound— she glanced again at the black-and-white picture on the comforter —*and that I had to give you a chance at life. But I never expected to love you, right from the first moment I saw you. Not like this.*

I guess that's why I didn't understand when Dr. Allen warned me how hard it would be to give you up. I thought I did, but I was wrong. It's like I know in my head I'm too young to be your mother, but my heart keeps saying, "Yes you could!"

Nikki blinked hard, several times, then pulled a tissue from the box on the table by her bed and blew her nose.

At least the Shiveleys will be a better family for you than mine would. They're both close to their parents, so you'll have grandparents that really care about you. Like Evan, the four-year-old back in Ohio I used to babysit. He's the one I named you after, and I was so glad when Marilyn and Jim chose to keep that name. I always thought that Evan was such a neat name, and that someday, if I ever got to have a baby of my own, that's what I would call him. Anyway, Evan and Lindy, his sister, used to talk about their grandparents all the time.

And I always got to come and spend the summer with Gram and Grandpa every year, so I know how special grandparents can be. I know it hurts them, too, that they'll never really get to know you, Evan, but you have to understand, I couldn't ask them to raise you, not with Gram's stroke and all. And your real grandparents—my mother and dad—well, they just didn't want anything to do with you. Or even with me, as long as I was pregnant.

She glanced uneasily at the dresser drawer where her mother's letter lay, unopened, and listened to the wind rattle the windowpane. She could tell by the scouring, scratching sound in each gust of wind against the side of the house that the soft, fluffy snowflakes must have given way to tiny icy ones.

They didn't want to see us, or talk to us, or anything. And no matter what, I'll make sure they don't.

❧ *Four* ❧

NIKKI FELL ASLEEP without putting the phone back in the hall, and when it rang next to her ear, the sound startled her out of a deep sleep. She fumbled for the receiver and squinted at the cold, gray light that filled the room.

"H'lo?"

"Nikki? Is that you? This is Jeff." There was a pause. "I'm not calling too early, am I?" He sounded anxious, a little unsure of himself.

Nikki slid down farther beneath the thick comforter before she answered. "Hi. What time is it?"

"Eight o'clock on your side of the lake, seven over here. I just wanted to make sure you're all right."

Nikki gave a huge yawn and tried to bury the sound with her hand. "Why wouldn't I be all right?"

"Well, you never called back last night."

"Oh. Uh, I got home too late." *Technically, that's a lie,* she thought, *but just barely. I only had 15 minutes by the time Grandpa finished talking to me.*

"I thought you said you were going to play practice."

"Well, yeah, I did. But we changed our minds. I mean, one of the guys in the play got tickets to the Black Tail Spin concert in Columbia, so we went to that instead."

Jeff hesitated for a second. "Someone I know?"

"Jeff, don't talk crazy. Who would you know in this school except me?"

"Besides," he answered, "when did you get into headbanger music, anyway? You don't even like that kind of stuff."

Nikki pulled the receiver away from her head and frowned at it. Then she put it back against her ear. "And since when do you know everything there is to know about me?"

There was silence on the other end of the line, and Nikki had a clear image of the hurt in his dark-blue eyes. "Oh, Jeff, I'm sorry. And you're right, I usually don't like that kind of music—"

"No," he broke in, "*you're* right. I'm the one who's sorry. I mean, really, it's none of my business what you did last night, right?"

The conversation limped along after that, both of them testing each word awkwardly.

Nikki could hardly hear what he said over the thoughts spinning wildly in her head. *You've always been there when I needed you, Jeff—last summer when I was going crazy trying to decide about an abortion. And all those summers we spent next door to each other up here at the lake, you and Carly and me—we were a team.* But all she said was, "So, do you have a game today?"

"Nope. We finally got a break. Actually, that's another reason I was calling, Nik. We have Monday off. The teachers have some in-service day or something. You do, too, don't you?"

Nikki lifted her freezing feet and let the comforter drape around and underneath them. "That's right. I forgot all about that."

"Well, I thought maybe I'd drive up tonight and kind of hang around for the rest of the weekend. It's been so cold, Dad thought I should check the pipes in our house up there." He hesitated. "Maybe that's not such a good idea."

Chad's image flashed across her mind, and she tried to think of how she could keep Jeff from meeting him. "Uh, sure," she said aloud. "C'mon up. I know Gram and Grandpa will be glad to see you. And me, too, of course. What about Carly? Is she coming?"

"Nah, she's got the flu. She hasn't been out of bed since Thursday, except to throw up. Listen, I better get off the phone. I'll be there sometime after dinner, then."

Nikki hung up and burrowed back underneath the thick, warm covers. But try as she would, she couldn't fall back asleep. After half an hour, she gave up, flung the comforter and blankets aside, and reached for her sweatpants and slippers.

As she made her way down the stairs, yawning and rubbing her eyes, Grandpa was just turning the corner into his study.

"Morning!" she called to him, and he looked back over the shoulder of his red plaid flannel shirt, surprised, and held his coffee mug up in salute.

"What are you doing up so early on a Saturday?" he asked. "That phone call keep you from going back to sleep?"

Nikki nodded and yawned again. "Jeff's coming up tonight for the weekend. They have Monday off school like we do, so he's coming to check on their house."

"And maybe get in a little time with a certain girl I know?"

"Oh, c'mon, Grandpa. He's just coming to take care of the house."

Grandpa grinned and sipped his coffee. "If that's what you say. Just seems a little funny to me. The Allens have owned that house next door for 18 years, and I've looked after it all those winters while they were back in Chicago."

Nikki shrugged. "Where are you going? You're usually getting breakfast for Gram right now."

Grandpa rolled his eyes and put a finger to his lips. In their silence, Nikki could hear voices from the kitchen—Gram's low, halting words, then a loud, sharp, fast-moving voice that seemed to flow on and on without a break.

"Arleta's here?" she whispered. "*This early?*"

Grandpa nodded, then disappeared into the study with a wave.

Arleta was a neighbor and one of Gram's best friends. She was also secretary of the town counsel, volunteer for the American Cancer Society, the Heart Fund, and other medical groups too numerous to mention, chairperson of the annual bowl-a-thon for Muscular Dystrophy, and the Rosendale librarian, a job where she read every issue of *Health Update* from cover to cover and regularly misquoted everything she read. She loved to help and she loved to talk, though it seemed to Nikki she did more of the latter than the former.

Nikki took the long way to the kitchen, through the living room and dining room, and stopped there to take in the view from the huge bay window. There were at least four inches of new snow tracing each spidery black tree branch and quilting the frozen lake beyond. A little black-capped nuthatch clung to the edge of the bird feeder, nosing its tiny sharp beak over and over into the snow where the seed and suet should be but coming up empty each time.

Nikki pushed open the window and brushed the feeder clean, grimacing at the cold of the snow on her bare hand. The bird flew away in panic, but she knew it would be back within minutes, anxious for its meal. The sky was still a sullen, brooding ceiling of gray, as though it hadn't yet gotten all the bad weather out of its system. Nikki took a deep breath, steeling herself, and walked on toward the kitchen.

"Good morning, Gram. Morning, Arleta," she began, but even that got chopped off in the flow of Arleta's words, which changed direction as effortlessly as the stream from a fireman's hose.

"WELL, LOOK WHO'S HERE!"

She could walk into the room a hundred times a day, Nikki thought, and Arleta would still say "Well, look who's here!" every single time.

"I DIDN'T EXPECT TO SEE SOMEONE YOUR AGE UP THIS EARLY IN THE MORNING."

Arleta made it sound as though being 17 was a peculiar kind of handicap that kept people in bed long past the acceptable rising time.

Arleta stood no more than five feet tall and probably weighed less than 90 pounds soaking wet, but her tongue was Olympic material for sure, Nikki thought. The little white-haired woman made a clucking sound with her tongue—Arleta was a great clucker, and even her *clucks* were louder than most people's normal conversation—and pulled another section of Gram's gray hair taut between the ends of a white paper square. She wound it around a spindly, pink plastic curler and snapped the curler securely into place.

Arleta was always anxious to try different hairdos on people, though Nikki had observed that she never experimented on herself. As Nikki grabbed a bagel from the counter and popped it in the toaster, she prepared herself for the next cascade of words.

"I WAS JUST TELLING YOUR GRAM—WHO'S FEELING PRETTY CHIPPER THIS MORNING, BY THE WAY—" Arleta squeezed one of Gram's shoulders with her bony fingers and stepped carefully around Gallie, who sat beside Gram's chair "—THAT THE NEWS SAID THE SNOW CAUSED EIGHT ACCIDENTS ALREADY THIS MORNING."

Nikki nodded and opened her mouth to answer, but it was a

false alarm. Arleta had no intention of making a full stop.

"REMEMBER THAT 10-CAR PILEUP IN THE ICE STORM, CAROLE? ABOUT 20 YEARS AGO?"

She shook her head and went on without waiting for a reply. "YOU JUST NEVER KNOW WHAT'LL HAPPEN IN THE WINTER AROUND HERE. GET A LITTLE ICE ON THOSE ROADS AND FIRST THING YOU KNOW, YOU'RE IN THE LAKE." One bony arm—clad in the sleeve of a purple warm-up suit, which was coordinated with dangling purple earrings and purple socks—shot out into the air, tracing the trajectory of a hapless car on Michigan ice.

Arleta had recently discovered color analysis—about a decade later than the rest of the country, Nikki thought—and she lived faithfully by its rules. Just from looking at her today, Nikki could tell purple must be a premium color for "winters."

"I REMEMBER JUST A FEW YEARS AGO THAT FAMILY FROM INDIANA THAT HIT SOME ICE AND WENT RIGHT OVER THE BANK. IT TOOK NEARLY ALL DAY FOR THE FIRE-MEN TO GET THAT CAR BACK UP ON THE ROAD. THEY HAD TO BRING IN A CRANE!"

Nikki took her bagel out of the toaster and spread it with cream cheese. She barely got one bite into her mouth when the stench of ammonia filled the air. She'd forgotten just how bad a home perm could smell. She chewed slowly, swallowed once, then pushed the plate away from her and tried to drink her orange juice before the fumes flavored that, too.

Arleta was finally silent for a few seconds because she had bobby pins in her mouth so that both her hands were free to soak each hair-filled roller on Gram's head with the perm solution. Nikki saw her chance and took it.

"Gram, Jeff called this morning. He's going to drive up tonight and stay at their house till sometime Monday. His dad wants him to check the pipes and everything. . . ."

Gram barely had time to smile when Arleta broke in, her mouth now free of pins.

"JEFF ALLEN! NOW THERE'S A GOOD-LOOKING BOY. WELL, REALLY, I SHOULD SAY YOUNG MAN, THE WAY HE GREW UP THIS LAST YEAR. REMEMBER HOW HE USED TO BE SO CHUBBY, NIKKI? AND HE WORE THOSE GLASSES THAT WERE ALWAYS SLIDING DOWN HIS NOSE?"

Arleta tied the ends of the plastic cap over Gram's forehead and stood back to admire her handiwork, her bright brown eyes shiny and intent. With her compact body and constant quick movements, Arleta reminded Nikki of the nuthatch at the bird feeder.

Peck, peck, peck, all day long, from the minute she wakes up till the minute she falls asleep. Except for her volume level. There all similarity to a small bird ended. She had the volume of a particularly loud crow at dawn.

Arleta was off and running again. "JEFF'S ALWAYS BEEN A NICE BOY, A REAL GENTLEMAN, EVEN THOUGH HE WASN'T MUCH TO LOOK AT FOR A LONG TIME. CARLY, NOW SHE'S A DIFFERENT STORY. PRETTY AS A PICTURE, BUT FLIGHTY. THAT'S WHAT MY MOTHER WOULD HAVE CALLED CARLY. THE GIRL OWED ME EIGHT DOLLARS AND CHANGE ON OVERDUE BOOKS AND MAGAZINES BY THE TIME THE ALLENS LEFT TO GO BACK TO CHICAGO IN SEPTEMBER.

"'PRETTY IS AS PRETTY DOES' MY MOTHER ALWAYS USED TO SAY, THOUGH I SUPPOSE IT SHOULD BE '*HAND-SOME* IS AS *HANDSOME* DOES' IN JEFF'S CASE, RIGHT, NIKKI?"

Arleta chuckled at her own wit, pulled the hood of the old

stand dryer down to Gram's forehead and switched it on low. Then she raised her voice even further to compensate for the hum, and Gallie lay down at Gram's side and lowered his soft golden head behind her legs as though to hide his ears.

"I HEAR MARLENE AND DR. ALLEN WERE A BIG HELP, NIKKI, WHEN YOU HAD TO CHOOSE THE PARENTS FOR YOUR BABY." She held out a cup toward Gram. "HERE, CAROLE, A NICE, HOT CUP OF TEA FOR YOU. ARE YOU SURE YOU CAN HOLD IT ALL RIGHT UNDER THERE?"

Nikki flinched. She hated it when Arleta tried to pry. *At least I won't have to say anything,* she thought. *She never waits for an answer anyway.* Nikki got up and carried her dish and glass to the sink. She wanted to get out of the kitchen before Arleta went any further with this subject. She stepped on the foot pedal of the blue waste-basket and the top flew open. Gallie, always interested in the trash can, bounded to her side from his seat by Gram's chair.

"YOU'RE NOT THROWING AWAY THE REST OF THAT BAGEL!" cried Arleta, who could never stand the slightest hint of waste. "WHY, YOU HARDLY TOUCHED IT! WHY DON'T YOU JUST WRAP IT IN SOME FOIL AND TUCK IT RIGHT AWAY IN THE FRIDGE THERE, RIGHT NEXT TO THAT NICE LASAGNA I BROUGHT OVER FOR YOUR DINNER?"

Nikki sighed and reached for the aluminum foil. Gallie, seeing the wastebasket lid fall, hung his head and padded back to Gram's side.

"ANYWAY, I JUST THINK IT WAS PROVIDENTIAL THAT THE ALLENS TURNED OUT TO BE SUCH A BIG HELP TO YOU. YOU CAN'T HAVE TOO MANY FRIENDS WHEN TIMES ARE ROUGH, I ALWAYS SAY."

She turned toward Carole Nobles. "JUST LIKE WHEN RACHEL FOUND OUT—ABOUT ROGER, I MEAN."

Found out what? Nikki wondered, but the question was gone the instant she thought it because Gram's cup tumbled from her hands with a crash and the sound of splintering pottery. Both Arleta and Nikki jumped into action, armed with paper towels and dishcloths.

"Did it burn you?" Nikki cried, trying to sponge the brown liquid off of Gram's slippers. "Are you hurt?"

"No." Gram shook her head, licking her lips, but Nikki noticed that her face was pale. "No, I'm fine. Just my . . . slippers."

Nikki pulled the stained slippers off her grandmother's feet and felt inside them, but the hot liquid had not penetrated their soft fleece lining.

It wasn't until much later, after Nikki had escaped both the ammonia smell and the unbroken tide of Arleta's conversation to work on Spanish homework in her bedroom, that she remembered the comment about her mother.

But no amount of curiosity could drive Nikki back downstairs to endure more of Arleta's endless chatter.

By early afternoon, Nikki had waded through two chapters of Spanish—she was still behind from taking off two weeks when she had the baby—and a book report for Mr. Keaton on *Pride and Prejudice*.

She was putting the finished report into her notebook when the doorbell rang. Nikki went to the top of the stairs and saw Grandpa emerge from the study, his white hair standing on end from his habit of running his hand through it, over and over, as he wrote. Behind him, Arleta scurried in from the kitchen, eager to find out who was at the door.

It was Keesha Riley, her hands and head muffled in thick,

wool mittens and scarf, with her brother's plaid lumberjack coat wrapped around her bulky form. She unwound the scarf from her hair and stooped to pull off her boots.

Nikki giggled inside as she watched Arleta's eyes light up in fascination at the grid of skinny, beaded cornrow braids that covered Keesha's bent head. *Lucky Gram's hair isn't long enough for Arleta to try that one.*

"I'm up here," she called, and Keesha peered up the stairs.

"Hey, Nik! Man, I felt like a freight train plowing through all that snow." She patted her belly, prominent in the too-snug pink jumpsuit. Bold black lettering across the top proclaimed "BABY" and a black arrow pointed to the unmistakable location.

As though anybody could miss it! Nikki thought.

Arleta's eyes opened wide as she watched Nikki's friend, then they grew even wider as Keesha spoke again. "Two more weeks and I get to unload Junior here."

Nikki flinched. She knew she needed to get Keesha out of the front hall immediately. It wasn't hard to remember how tight-lipped Arleta had been when she first found out Nikki was pregnant—it was the only time she'd ever seen her completely at a loss for words. Little by little, the older woman had accepted the situation and was now as garrulous and full of advice as ever toward her friend's granddaughter. But then, Nikki had always worn loose, baggy clothes and never voluntarily brought up the subject around Arleta.

Keesha, on the other hand, had never had a secret in her life. *If Arleta's a nuthatch,* Nikki thought, *then Keesha's a blue jay—loud, to the point, and a little bit brash.*

"Sorry I'm late," Keesha went on, looking up at Nikki.

"Late for what?" Nikki asked.

"Late for *what?*" Keesha echoed. She clamped her hands

where her waist used to be, elbows akimbo. "That's just great! I plow through half a mile of blizzard to get here and you don't even remember why I came, do you?" She turned to Arleta and Grandpa. "Got a mind like a steel trap, that girl. Tell her something important and just like that—" she snapped her fingers "—it's gone forever." She glanced at Nikki, her eyes narrowed. "You don't remember that Keaton expects us to come up with some costumes for *The Glass Menagerie*?"

She turned back to Grandpa and Arleta. "He couldn't figure out any parts for Nikki and me, since we were both pregnant and all, so he told us to do costumes and props together. Nikki said you might have some old clothes up in the attic we could look through."

"We have old clothes, all right, from the last 40 years or so. You'll do us a favor if you clean some of it out." Grandpa took Keesha's coat and scarf and hung them up in the hall closet.

"That's good," Keesha said, "'cause he's really breathing down our necks to get this stuff. I don't know who's taking up more of my time anymore, old Keaton with his play or Junior here. Keaton barks orders and expects us all to drop everything else and snap to it, and I can't do that with the baby growing like a weed."

"How's he doing these days, with the deadline getting so close?" Grandpa asked.

Keesha looked at him innocently. "Just like you'd expect— twisting and kicking and keeping me up all night, every night."

"HONESTLY!" Arleta said.

But Grandpa laughed out loud and said, "No, no, I meant Nick Keaton and the deadline for his play. Nick was a student of mine years ago at Howellsville College."

"Oops!" Keesha laughed, then looked up to where Nikki stood. "Speaking of Keaton—*Mr.* Keaton, that is," she added with a sidelong look at Arleta and Grandpa, "he was really worried about Chad last night. Is it true that—?"

"Come on upstairs, Keesha," Nikki cut in hurriedly. "We can talk better up here. Come *on*."

❧ *Five* ❧

KEESHA SPRAWLED ACROSS THE BED, her breath coming fast after trudging up the stairs. "*Sheww!* At least at our house, everything's on one floor. How much longer can a person carry 35 extra pounds?"

"Probably about two weeks," Nikki said, "since that's when you're due."

"Boy, you're all sympathy, aren't you? So what's the deal with Chad? Why didn't you want me to mention his accident in front of them?" She nodded toward the stairs.

"Because there *wasn't* any accident. But you have to promise not to tell anybody that," Nikki added quickly.

"*What?* Why would Keaton tell us that Chad's dad said . . . ? Wait a minute. You mean Chad got somebody to call and pretend to be his father? And *lie* for him?"

"Well, yeah. Except he didn't need anybody to call for him. You know how he's always doing all those voices? Well, he called Mr. Keaton himself."

"But *why?*"

"Because he got us tickets to the Black Tail Spin concert in

Columbia last night, so he had to get out of play practice."

"No way! That concert was sold out a month ago. Where'd he get tickets?"

Nikki shrugged. "He wouldn't tell me."

Keesha's eyes narrowed as she stared up at the ceiling. "I don't know about Chad, Nikki. He's gorgeous, sure, but I don't trust him. He's just too slick. I mean, here we were, worried sick about him last night. And it was all a lie. It's almost as though he *wants* to hurt people, you know?"

They were silent for a minute, then Keesha's voice grew serious. She cradled her stomach in her hands and looked at Nikki, who was curled up on the window seat. "Speaking of hurt, I've been wanting to ask you about . . . things. Like labor. Was it really as bad as they say?"

Nikki hesitated. "Well, it's no picnic. But—" she hurried on when she saw the look on Keesha's face "—they give you all kinds of medicine to help. When it got bad, they gave me something called a block, and I was numb from the waist down but still awake so I could see everything."

Keesha struggled to a sitting position. "How'd they give it to you? A shot?"

"Yeah."

She groaned and put her face in her hands.

"It didn't hurt," Nikki said quickly. "Not much, anyway."

"Listen, baby, there's no such thing as a shot that doesn't hurt. I *hate* needles."

"It's not as bad as you think, Keesha. And once it's over, you just kind of put it out of your mind." Nikki looked down at her hands and began forcing back the cuticle on each nail. "The really hard part is coming home without the baby. At least *you* won't have to do that."

"You're having a hard time with it, aren't you, Nik?"

Nikki nodded and went on working on her hands. She didn't dare look up at Keesha for fear the tears pooled in her eyes would overflow.

"Man, there's no way I could do that." Keesha's voice was softer than Nikki had ever heard it. "My mom would have a fit, too. She was really mad at first when I told her I was pregnant, but now she's got part of my room all fixed up with my old crib and stuff. I think she's more excited than I am."

Nikki finished her last nail and drew her knees up to her chest, her arms locked around them. "Keesha, did you ever think about . . . about having an abortion?"

Keesha pushed herself up off the bed and walked across the rose-colored carpet to Nikki's dresser. She began searching through the earrings in her open jewelry box as though she hadn't heard the question.

"Well? Did you?" Nikki asked.

Keesha picked up a pair of red-and-white Chicago Cubs buttons Carly had made into earrings and given to Nikki as a joke years ago, when she and Jeff were still trying to get her to cheer their favorite team.

"Why would I do a stupid thing like that?" Keesha answered finally. Then she leaned against the dresser, peering at the snapshot stuck into the frame of Nikki's mirror and changed the subject quickly. Too quickly, Nikki thought. "Hey, who's the guy?"

"Just a friend. Jeff Allen."

"Whoa! Let's have some details here. Just because I look like a beached whale these days doesn't mean I can't appreciate the natural beauty all around me."

Nikki laughed. "Like I said, he's just a friend. His family spends the summer up here every year in the house next door.

He's a year older than me and his sister Carly is a year younger, and we've been friends since we were in diapers. And they have a little brother and sister who are twins, and their dad's a surgeon in Chicago." She took a long breath. "There, are you satisfied now?"

Keesha put her hands on her hips. "You're holding out on me, girl!"

"I am not," Nikki protested.

"Oh, yeah? Then how come *his* picture's on your mirror and not his sister's? If they're all just *friends*, like you say."

"Because Carly thought I'd like to see a picture of Jeff making the winning basket of the game, that's all."

Keesha grinned at her knowingly.

"Fine!" Nikki said. "You can meet him yourself. He's coming up here tonight."

"I'll look forward to that, for sure," Keesha said. She held out the oversized earrings to Nikki. "Here, put these on."

"I don't want to wear those things—they're huge!"

"No, they're great. I think they're really cool," Keesha insisted. "Put them on. I want to see how they look."

"Okay, okay. But then we'd better get upstairs and get to work in the attic."

"**O**oohh, Nik, look what I found!" Keesha pulled a pair of round-toed black heels from a trunk. "Can you believe anybody ever wore these? Here, try them on and see if they fit."

Nikki took the shoes from her and inspected them. The heels were thick and chunky, with a wide, black button strap across the front. "Why me? Why don't you try them on?"

"Number one, because your feet are about the same size as the star of our show's, while mine—" Keesha looked down at her swollen feet encased in hot-pink slouch socks and pouted "—are about the same size as your average elephant's, give or take an inch. So if you can wear them, Jen can wear them. You got that? And number two, because the doctor says no heels till the baby's born. Sheesh! It's only been a month and you forgot all this already? I don't think I'll *ever* forget."

"Don't worry. Nobody forgets those parts." Nikki kicked off her slippers and slid the shoes on over her bare feet. She stuck her legs out in front of her and winced. "Boy, they're awful, aren't they?"

"Hey, we're talking authentic '40s here. Anyway, put 'em in the pile of stuff to show Keaton."

Nikki surveyed the attic. So far they'd opened four boxes and two trunks and made a gigantic mess. Clothes and books and shoes were strewn in haphazard piles. She dropped to her knees in front of the last trunk. The latch was unlocked, and she eased up the heavy lid. The top tray held several pieces of costume jewelry they could probably use for the play, but as she started looking through them, Keesha cried, "Hey, Nik, look at this!"

Nikki leaned back, her hands behind her on the floor, and watched as Keesha held up a red coatdress, bulky with shoulder pads and huge black buttons, against her pink jumpsuit and pretended to model it. "Awesome, huh?" Keesha asked. "Especially with my figure. You know, I kind of like these clothes. Maybe I should've been born 50 years ago, what do you think?"

"I don't know," Nikki answered. "I think it would have been harder for both of us if we were born that long ago. I think you had to drop out of school if you got pregnant back then." She looked up at her friend, who was still admiring herself in the red dress. "Keesha, do you ever worry about things? Like not finishing school because you're keeping the baby? Or about what you'll tell your baby when it asks about a father?"

Keesha shrugged. "I turned out all right without a father, didn't I, so what's the big deal? And who says I won't finish school? You never met my family, Nik, but I have four older sisters and a brother. There'll always be somebody around to watch the baby. That's how we do things at my house. Like I told you about my mom—she yelled and carried on and told me I was grounded for the rest of my life when she first found out. But I knew she'd calm down. She always does."

Nikki sighed, remembering the day her mother and father drove her to the doctor's office for the abortion. She could still see her mother smoothing on her lipstick, her face reflected in the vanity mirror on the back of the sun visor like a pale, carefully-controlled, emotionless mask.

"My mother doesn't yell and carry on. Not much, anyway. But she doesn't calm down either. It's just different at my house, Keesha. I don't think you could ever understand my family."

"Try me," Keesha urged.

"Well, my dad's an attorney. He's always off meeting clients or working on cases. He used to play with me when I was really little—I can still remember that. But once his practice took off, everything changed. And my mother never really had much time for anything but her music—she teaches at a junior college by our house back in Ohio and sings in an opera company. So I kind of just . . . got in the way. Besides, when my parents do have time at home, they mostly spend it fighting with each other."

Keesha eased herself down onto an old chair, the red coatdress around her knees.

"Dad was afraid that if anyone found out I was pregnant, he wouldn't get this judgeship he's been dying for," Nikki went on. "And Mother didn't want people to know because it could spoil her career. Millbrook's still a small place and pretty uptight about things like that—and news travels fast. So they decided I was having an abortion and that was that."

"Get out of here!" Keesha said. "They tried to *make* you have an abortion?"

"Yeah. Things didn't work out like they planned, though. But when I told them I was going to go ahead and have the baby, they just walked out and went back to Ohio. And said not to come home pregnant."

Keesha sighed. "Life stinks sometimes, doesn't it?" Then she glanced at her watch and hoisted herself to her feet. "Nikki, listen, I've got to go. I told my mom I'd be home by four and it's already four-thirty. I'll have to come back another day and help you clean this all up. What are you doing Monday?"

Nikki closed the lid of the trunk and looked around the room. "Something tells me I'm working right here! Listen, do you want me to drive you home? I'll borrow my grandparents' car."

Keesha crossed the attic to look out the small, dusty window in the eaves. "Nah, the roads have all been plowed, it looks like. And I've gotta get some exercise. All the doctor ever says to me anymore is, 'Walk, walk, walk! You're beginning to look like a barrel.'"

The snow started up again as Nikki sliced Arleta's steaming lasagna into squares. When she pulled the knife out of the noodles, long strings of melted mozzarella clung to it. She lifted the knife higher, then higher still, trying to break the strands of cheese, and could see Gram's eyes laughing as she watched.

"Your arms need to be a foot longer," she said.

Nikki pulled the strands of cheese off the knife with her fingers and popped them in her mouth. "At least there's one thing Arleta can do without talking—make a terrific lasagna." She inhaled the rich, yeasty aroma of Grandpa's hot rolls—"homemade, straight from the can," he always joked.

A sudden gust of icy wind off the lake sent a burst of snowflakes swirling against the bay window, and Grandpa got up from the table and pulled down the window shade, shutting out the bleak winter light. "Looks like a good night for the fireplace. What do you say, Carole? Want to sit in front of a nice, roaring fire with me later?"

Gram nodded and smiled across the table at him, and Nikki thought how much the scene reminded her of those pages in the children's magazines she got years ago, the ones titled, "WHAT'S WRONG WITH THIS PICTURE?"

At first the drawings always looked completely normal, and you couldn't find anything out of place. But then, when you looked closer, you spotted a turkey in the fishbowl or people eating dinner with skis strapped onto their bare feet.

She looked around at the old corner hutch that shone like satin from years of polishing, at the heavy, cherry-red pottery plates on the table and the hardwood floor covered here and there with knobby hand-woven rugs, and she thought how cozy it should feel.

But I can't remember feeling good about much of anything for a long time now.

She thought about the wild excitement of running down the beach to Lake Michigan when she used to come for summer vacations. There had been long, rambling walks with Gallie under the thick canopy of oaks and maples that covered the dunes, and magical evenings on the pier, watching the bobbing lights of boats headed home into the channel. Leaving the flat, featureless landscape around her home in Ohio and coming here always made her feel like a bird let out of its cage. Until this year.

It's as though being pregnant, and then giving Evan away, used up all my feelings. And now there's nothing left. Except anger. Nikki's lips tightened, and she cut into her lasagna with her fork.

Nikki watched her grandmother, gray hair neatly curled with Arleta's latest ministrations, struggle to break a roll in half. After months of therapy, her left hand was just beginning to work again.

Grandpa noticed her efforts and automatically reached out to help. Nikki saw the flash in Gram's eyes that passed between them and grinned inwardly as her grandfather withdrew his hand. No one pitied Gram and got away with it.

Nikki picked up her own roll then and broke it neatly in two, watching her hands as she buttered a piece. And suddenly she understood that even though her body appeared to work perfectly on the outside, something inside her was far more damaged than Gram's hand.

❧ *Six* ❧

IT WAS LATE IN THE EVENING by the time Jeff wheeled the red Bronco into the driveway between the Allens' house and the blue clapboard that belonged to her grandparents.

Gram and Grandpa had already had their roaring fire, and Nikki had done her part by making a teapot full of hot chocolate for them, with some saved back for Jeff and herself. The fire was burning low, and Nikki was peering out the front window for at least the tenth time before she saw the high headlights of the Bronco nosing down the snowy street.

"Jeff's here!" she called out, and hurried back through the house to unlock the kitchen door.

In the yellow glow of the porch light, Jeff's boots left footprints three inches deep on the back steps Grandpa had shoveled clean just before dinner. The wind hurled some of the new snow through the open doorway, and Jeff ducked his head and stepped inside quickly so Nikki could close the door behind him.

"*Whew!* What a trip," he said, unsnapping his maroon letter jacket and pushing back the hood of the sweatshirt he wore underneath.

Nikki was almost speechless when she saw his head uncovered. She knew from pictures that Jeff had his hair cropped short each year for basketball season. But this time, he was nearly bald.

"What happened?" she gasped, then tried to rephrase that quickly when she saw his embarrassment. "I mean, your hair. What—?"

"It was a tournament thing." Jeff shrugged. "You know, all the guys on the team shaved their heads. . . . Kind of stupid, I guess, huh?"

As she watched him, Nikki thought how much more prominent his strong cheekbones looked this way. Even his long-lashed, dark-blue eyes seemed to stand out more.

Jeff ran both hands across his head and gave her a lopsided grin. "Haven't had a bad hair day ever since I got it shaved, though."

Nikki shook her head, laughing. "You know, the weird thing is, I kind of like it." It was the first time she'd seen Jeff since his nighttime visit to the hospital with flowers, and a moment's awkwardness lay between them. Jeff broke it with a laugh of his own, staring at her ears.

"Great earrings, Nik! I always figured we'd get you converted to being a Cubs fan sooner or later."

Nikki realized she was still wearing the Chicago Cubs earrings Keesha had made her try on earlier in the day. "Darn! I forgot all about them!" She reached up and took off the earrings as Jeff slid his arms out of the letter jacket and hung it on the coat tree by the kitchen door. Suddenly, they were back, comfortably, on their old footing.

Jeff brushed his faded blue sweatshirt down over dark jeans and followed her through the house to the living room, where her grandparents still sat in front of the dying fire.

An hour later, after they had caught up on the news of both families, Grandpa stood and offered Gram his arm. "I think it's bedtime, sweetheart."

Nikki sat cross-legged on the floor in front of the fireplace after her grandparents left. She held Jeff's mug of hot chocolate while he stirred up the embers and positioned one small, spindly log in the center of the grate.

"Just one little piece of wood here—don't want this thing to burn all night," Jeff explained as he arranged it, then dropped to the floor beside her, his long arms hugging his legs against his chest.

She handed his mug back to him and they sat side by side in silence, watching as tiny blue flames licked against the log, curving themselves to its sides, then swelled in seconds to a fiery orange. Jeff wiped a streak of soot from his forefinger, then balled up his paper napkin and shot it, with a careful snap of the wrist, into the exact center of the fire.

The flames flickered into little points of yellow, blue, and orange, and Nikki, growing sleepy in the fire's warmth, stared at the constantly changing colors.

When Jeff finally spoke, Nikki realized with a start that she'd been lost in her own thoughts long enough for the fire to take firm hold and snap and hiss its way through half the log.

That never would have happened if it had been Chad sitting here, she thought. Chad was a lot of things, but comfortable wasn't one of them. Jeff, on the other hand, had been around for so many summers that Nikki had to remind herself sometimes just how good a friend he was. She tried to focus her thoughts on what he was telling her about the basketball team and the winning streak they'd been on.

As the flames ate their way through the rest of the log with a subdued crackling and an occasional loud *pop*, Nikki told him about the Howellsville High School production of *The Glass Menagerie*, carefully leaving out any reference to Chad.

"Keesha's coming over again on Monday morning," she finished, "so we can go through the rest of the stuff in the attic. Mr. Keaton really needs props and costumes. This school doesn't exactly have a huge budget for drama."

Jeff drained the last of his hot chocolate before he spoke again. "You should have seen Carly this afternoon. She was really ticked that she couldn't come. She dragged herself out of bed while I was getting ready and swore she felt a million times better. 'Course, she was white as a sheet and had to lean against the wall just to stay upright, but you know Carly."

Nikki laughed and set her mug on the carpet beside her. "I know. She called me after you left, and she was spitting mad." She imitated Carly's voice. "'I am *too* better! I feel every bit as good as he does!'"

"That's exactly what she told my parents," Jeff replied. "Mom finally marched her back to bed and ordered her to stay there or else."

He stared into the dying fire for a few minutes, and when he spoke again his voice was soft. "Ever notice how sitting in front of a fire like this makes you think about things you don't usually have time for?"

Nikki felt her shoulders stiffen. It had taken all her effort in the last half hour just to hold her own thoughts at bay, but Jeff—being Jeff—always had to *think* about things, figure them out. It was one of the things she used to like best about him, but now she cringed at what was coming.

If he talks about Evan, I think I'll scream. Or if he brings up my parents . . .

But what Jeff actually said caught her so much off guard that

Nikki listened in spite of herself.

"I'll tell you what, driving through a snowstorm in the dark, by yourself, is just about the loneliest thing in the world. You ever feel like that?"

Nikki gave a little shrug. "I don't usually drive around in snowstorms too much."

"Well, I didn't mean that's the only time I'm ever lonely. It's just that there's usually so much going on, I don't think about it until I get into a situation where there're no distractions, like on the drive up here. Then it's like I realize that, way down inside, I've always been lonely for something. But I didn't know what for."

Nikki raised her eyebrows, and Jeff tried again, his fingers spread wide, emphasizing each point in the air in front of him. "Okay, listen. Forget about being lonely. It's like . . . like everybody in the world wants something. Only they never really know exactly what it is—they just keep finding out what it's *not*. You know how, when you turn off the TV, or you come out of some concert, and everything just feels . . . empty? Like you thought that would be what you wanted, and then it wasn't? Take Christmas, for example. It took me 15 years just to figure out that no matter how much stuff I got, it'd never be enough, because *stuff* wasn't really what I wanted. I just thought it was."

Jeff continued on, his voice excited and intense. "Or, here's one. You know how you get all worked up about a trip some-place, and you think it'll be the greatest thing in your life? But once you get there, even if it's great for a while, sooner or later you find out that wasn't it either?"

Tears welled up in Nikki's eyes as he spoke, and she looked straight ahead very carefully so he wouldn't see. *Or you think that getting to hold your own child, your own baby, whenever you want will do it. But deep inside, you know that even that won't be enough, not forever.*

She pressed her lips together so tightly that her jaws ached, and anger started somewhere deep inside her, anger at Jeff for ripping away all her protective layers with just a few simple words.

He pushed at the glowing embers with the bronze poker before he spoke again. "It's like everybody's telling you, 'Do this, get this, this is what'll fill you up inside.' But all the time, there's this little voice in your head saying, 'No, it won't. You know this'll get old, too.' It's like we all have this secret nobody talks about, and we all just keep chasing stuff to fill up that . . . that *wanting* inside, and we know all the time that what we're chasing won't do it. Not really. Not for good."

He turned his head and looked at her, and Nikki could feel the intensity in his gaze. "I know a lot has happened to you this year, Nik. That's why I haven't said anything about this before, but you're not the only one who's been going through big changes. Remember when we talked up on the dune last summer? And you told me about the baby? Well, that got me thinking. You know my family's really into Christianity. I mean, I was practically raised inside a church. But God never seemed real to me. When you started asking me questions about abortion and all, I knew right away I didn't have real answers."

He thought for a moment, then continued. "And inside, I'd got to the place where I'd messed up so many times, I could hardly stand to look at myself in the mirror. I thought about it all last fall, and over Christmas I went away to this big retreat with a couple thousand other teenagers. Something happened there, Nik. God kind of moved in on my heart and—I don't know exactly how to say it—on that whole part of me that was so empty. And all of a sudden, all that wanting and loneliness inside started to get filled up. Does that make any sense to you?"

Nikki stared into the fireplace, trying not to betray what she was feeling. When she heard Gallie give a short, sharp bark, she scrambled to her feet quickly.

"Listen, I hate to break this up, Jeff, but Gallie needs out. I'll be back in a minute."

After that, it was easy to sidetrack the conversation. Jeff followed her into the kitchen, carrying the empty hot chocolate mugs, and Nikki took more than enough time to rearrange the nearly-full dishwasher to make room for them.

They had to wait by the kitchen door for Gallie, who had a passion for fresh snow and refused to come inside. The big dog tunneled his snout through the fluffy whiteness, sending showers of it flying. Then he flopped over on his back and rolled and wiggled ecstatically in the cold powder, all four legs flopping loosely in the air above him.

"That's my favorite, when he does that," Nikki said. "He doesn't care how silly he looks."

"So much snow, so little time!" Jeff leaned against the frame of the kitchen door, shaking his head at the dog's antics.

Gallie, usually so obedient, completely ignored their calls, commands, and then even threats. "No table scraps for a week if you don't get in here *right now!*" Nikki finally yelled at him, laughing helplessly. She turned to Jeff and shrugged. "Sorry, but he always does this when it snows. We'll just have to wait till he's ready to come in."

But secretly, she was grateful to the dog for putting an end to Jeff's serious talk.

❧ Seven ❧

BY THE TIME NIKKI GOT DOWNSTAIRS the next morning, she knew she'd missed church again. She used to go with her grandparents, during the summers she spent here, and there had always been a lot of bedtime prayers and Bible stories from both Gram and Grandpa when she was little.

But back in Ohio, Sunday had been a day for her parents to catch up on reading and work they brought home from the office, or to have lunch with friends or clients. So for most of the year, Nikki didn't give church a second thought.

She'd tried praying about a couple of things, too, the way Gram and Grandpa always seemed to, but she never got any answers—not even when she begged God, the whole year she was 11, to make her parents stop fighting all the time. If anything, the fighting got worse. After that, she'd pretty much given up on prayer.

Until Gram had her stroke, that is. Nikki had promised God then that she would start going to church again if He would let her grandmother live. It was the only thing she could think of to offer, since she wasn't exactly sure how to bargain with God.

Gram lived, and Nikki went to church . . . for a while. But ever since she'd signed Evan over to the Shiveleys, she hadn't much felt like going back.

Nikki paused for a second in the kitchen doorway, watching Gram, who sat at the kitchen table gazing out the window that overlooked the driveway between the Nobles's house and the Allens'. Gallie sat in what had become his accustomed place since the stroke—as close to Gram as he could get, his great golden head resting on her lap. Nikki stepped over the dog's tail and hugged her grandmother gently.

"Is Grandpa still at church?" she asked.

Gram nodded and smiled toward the window. "Jeff's shoveling," she said, forming each word carefully.

Nikki realized she'd been hearing a snow shovel scraping against blacktop for several minutes, and she hurried to the window. "I'm surprised he's out this early. We stayed up pretty late talking." She felt again the haunting feeling Jeff's words had started up inside her.

Nikki opened the kitchen door and a burst of cold air blew in, the smell of the snow tingling in her nostrils. "Hey! Good morning!" she called to him.

Jeff straightened up and leaned on his shovel, pushing the knit hat back off his forehead, his wide smile showing his cleft chin to advantage. "Finally got out of bed, huh?" he yelled. "Give me 10 minutes to finish, and I'll be in."

She turned to go back inside, but Jeff's voice stopped her.

"Nik! Got any more of that hot chocolate?"

"I might, if you do a good enough job!" she called back, then shut the door against the cold, bright air and went to switch on the gas under the tea kettle. "He'll be frozen by the time he's done,

Gram. Do you want some hot chocolate with us? Oh, that's right, you're not supposed to have caffeine, are you? How about some nice herbal tea?"

"Chocolate will be fine," Gram said with a determined look. "Thanks."

"Well, if you say so," Nikki answered, taking bacon out of the refrigerator and waffles from the freezer. She wrinkled her nose at the greasy feel of the bacon on her fingers as she separated the strips and spread them on paper towels. When the bacon was in the microwave, she popped waffles in the toaster and set the table.

By the time she finished, Jeff was already stomping his boots against the steps outside to knock off the snow.

"Hey, it smells great in here," he said as he pulled off his cap and hung it on the coat tree. "Got any extra for a starving shoveler?"

Nikki laughed. "Who let you out without food, anyway? I thought you died if you skipped breakfast." She watched as he folded his long body into the chair by Gram.

Jeff looked at her sheepishly. "I didn't exactly *skip* it."

"You already *ate?*" Nikki said, and stopped halfway to the table with his full plate in her hands.

"Yeah, but so what? That was two whole hours ago." He winked at Gram and reached out to take the steaming plate from Nikki. "I went to the early service and then stopped at Rosie's for some scrambled eggs on the way home."

As they ate, Nikki was surprised and delighted to see how easily he pulled Gram into their conversation and even how traces of her old sense of humor began to surface.

Jeff, who wanted to be a doctor like his father, plied Gram with questions about her therapy. "So you're using five-finger exercises at the piano to strengthen your hand, right? Did they give you exercises for your whole left side—your arm and leg and everything?"

Gram rolled her eyes. Nikki started to answer for her and was surprised when her grandmother's voice carried over her own.

"*Everything,*" the older woman echoed emphatically.

"She has to do a half hour of exercises twice a day," Nikki explained. "Grandpa helps her in the morning, and I usually take the afternoon shift. She rides the exercise bike in the living room for 10 minutes, then does all sorts of stretches with her arm and leg, then we help her practice on the stairs."

Nikki grinned. "Grandpa says she's his very own Jane Fonda. He keeps teasing her about making her first exercise video."

Jeff reached across the table and picked up two more crisp slices of bacon. "Sounds like you're in training for the Olympics."

Nikki opened her mouth, but Grandma broke in again. "Exercise is my *life,*" she said slowly, her lips working hard to form the words distinctly. But her eyes sparkled as she spoke, and both Jeff and Nikki burst out laughing.

Gallie thumped his tail against the floor at the sound, but only his dark-brown eyes moved, tracing every action of Jeff's and Nikki's hands that involved food. His head never left Gram's lap until Jeff held out a piece of his bacon. Then the dog was at his side in a flash, licking his lips for more of the meat he'd already gulped down.

"You know, for such a big dog, he can really move," Jeff said.

"He's been one happy animal since Gram came home from the hospital," Nikki said, pushing her last bit of waffle through the syrup on her plate. "Nothing else matters to him these days."

"Almost nothing," Gram corrected her, eyeing the dog with half a smile. "I play second fiddle to table scraps, for sure."

Nikki looked up in surprise. "Gram, that's the longest sentence I've heard you say. That was great." She turned to Jeff. "She's really working hard on her speech. The therapist says that's the hardest part for her because the stroke damaged the speech control center in her brain more than anything else. Besides the exercises, she has to work on saying all these different sounds every day and . . ."

There was a great sigh from Gram's side of the table. Nikki broke off in surprise and stared at her grandmother, who stared right back.

"*I* will tell him. If you let me," she added.

Nikki sat perfectly still, her mouth open, and Jeff ducked his head, laughing.

"You and Roger have to let me talk," Gram said slowly.

"They're finishing your sentences for you, huh?" Jeff asked, and Gram nodded with another sigh.

"Starting them, too," she said.

Nikki sat in amazement as she listened to her grandmother. *I've been trying to make it easier for her by saying the words she struggles with faster and clearer.* "But I thought I was helping you."

Gram smiled at her and reached across the table to cover Nikki's hand with her own wrinkled one. "You did help . . . so much. But I'm getting better."

"Families always try to do too much," Jeff said. "Dad says that's one of the biggest problems for stroke victims."

Now it was Jeff's turn to come under Gram's indignant stare.

"I am not a victim," she said flatly.

"She hates that word." Nikki launched into an explanation, then stopped. "I'm doing it again, huh?" she laughed.

Gram laughed, too, and nodded. "I hate that word," she echoed. Then she went on. "Don't forget, tomorrow is Grand Rapids." This time she motioned with her hand for Nikki to explain.

"Grandpa takes Gram into the therapy center in Grand Rapids once a month for a whole day. They check her progress, then give her new exercises or whatever she needs." She turned back to her grandmother. "Keesha's coming over, and we'll probably just hang around here, okay? I have the day off of school because of teacher in-service training, and Jeff does, too."

"I have to leave right after lunch tomorrow. I told my folks I'd be back for dinner." Jeff swallowed the last of the hot chocolate, then set the cup back on the table. "What d'you say we go for a walk, Nik? On the beach?"

"Now? In the snow? It's freezing out there."

"It's not bad, now that the wind's stopped. And the sun's coming out." He nodded toward the kitchen window.

Nikki thought again of all the feelings his words had awakened the night before, and she hesitated. Even her dreams about Evan had seemed more vivid and painful than usual after they talked.

"Well, I really ought to start something for lunch first, because by the time we get back, Grandpa will probably be home from church. I guess we'll eat the rest of Arleta's lasagna, right, Gram? I could just do a salad really quick, and then we can go, okay?" At least that gave her an excuse. *I can always tell him the lasagna's probably ready when I want to come back.*

Jeff scrubbed vegetables under the spigot for her, picking bits of sand off the leaf lettuce and working intently at tiny spots on the carrot skins. But when she handed him a stalk of broccoli, he held it in the air between them with one thumb and forefinger and looked at her in disgust, his upper lip curling.

"Look, Nikki, I don't like to complain, but didn't anybody ever tell you a salad's not a dumping ground? You can't stick this kind of junk into a perfectly good tossed salad."

Nikki stopped slicing the cucumber she held, her hands in midair. "Why not?"

"'Cause I don't like bizarre vegetables, that's why."

"*Bizarre vegetables? Broccoli?* What are you talking about, Jeff?

What is a *nonbizarre* vegetable, anyway?"

He opened the crisper drawer of the refrigerator and laid the stalk of broccoli gingerly inside. "You know, ordinary stuff. Corn, beans."

"Don't you dare put that back in the refrigerator, Jeff Allen! I want broccoli in my salad."

Jeff swiveled around and crouched, his arms outstretched, in front of the refrigerator, as though he was guarding an opposing player. "Over my dead body!"

Nikki rolled her eyes and went back to slicing the cucumber. "Fine. Who needs vitamin C? You might have heard of vitamin C somewhere before, huh? Or don't they go in for that kind of stuff in Chicago?"

"Oh, right, take potshots at my hometown. I don't think that's a politically correct thing to do anymore, ma'am."

Nikki waited until Jeff turned his back to scrub at another nonexistent blemish on the carrots, then she twisted the damp dish towel into a tight rope and turned silently, holding her breath, to snap it at him. But just as she prepared to let it fly, Jeff turned in a flash and caught her arm.

"AAHH!" she shrieked, so startled she dropped the towel. "How did you do that?"

"Hears all, sees all, knows all—that's me. You just keep that in mind." He stooped to pick up the towel and dangled it just out of her reach. "And remember who's got the towel, kiddo."

When the salad—minus broccoli—was covered and set in the refrigerator, and the lasagna was put in the oven to warm on low, Nikki and Jeff made their way down the snow-covered steps to the icy beach.

"I'm so bundled up I can hardly move," Nikki complained, pushing back her grandmother's knit hat that kept sliding down over her eyes.

"Mom used to make Carly and me wear snowsuits when we were little. You know those full-length jobs?" Jeff asked, and Nikki nodded. "I remember, she'd get so frustrated. It'd take her forever to get both of us all dressed up in those suits and boots and hats and mittens. And then we'd just barely get outside and one of us would have to go to the bathroom, every single time."

The ice over the rocks was sculpted into amazing whorls and swirls, little rounded hillocks alongside fantastic almost-figures that looked like something out of a science fiction movie. The sun had broken through the heavy gray clouds and glinted off its surface so that they had to squint in the brightness.

"Here, give me your hand!" Jeff called, as Nikki, balanced on one of the ice-covered rocks, started to slide forward and shrieked.

She threw out both hands toward him, and he caught her easily, then pretended to stagger backward.

"Whoa!" he cried. "How many waffles did you say you ate?"

And suddenly, everything was just like it used to be, before the pregnancy, before the baby. Nikki felt as though she was full of the bright sunshine, sparkling ice, and the blue, blue sky reflected in the water far out from shore, where the lake hadn't frozen over yet. She clambered up onto another little hill of snow and thrust her hand against her chest dramatically.

"Waffles are my life!" she proclaimed, and they both doubled over laughing. "Can you believe Gram said that? About exercise? That's the first time I've seen her even try to be funny since the stroke."

"She sure didn't sugarcoat it when she told you to stop doing her talking for her either, did she?" Jeff said. "That's gotta be a good sign. That she's getting back to normal, I mean."

"You know," Nikki said, "when I think how she looked the night she had the stroke, I can hardly believe she's even alive.

And Grandpa—I thought he'd die just from the pain of seeing her go through all that. That's why he waits on her hand and foot. They just . . . they just love each other so much. More than anybody else I know." Nikki stared out at the horizon for a minute. "Wouldn't that be a neat way to live your life? Anyway, I'm really excited about how fast Gram's getting better."

"We pray for her at home every day. For you, too, Nikki. You know that, don't you?"

Nikki gave a small half shrug. "Right," she said, but all at once, half the sparkle seemed gone from the day. "And I appreciate it." She found she couldn't leave it there, though, and turned to face him. "But I have to tell you, I don't really believe praying does any good anymore."

"What d'you mean?"

"Listen, Jeff, you know all those summers I spent up here with Gram and Grandpa? They were always taking me to church and saying prayers with me at bedtime and reading me Bible stories about all these fantastic things God does for people. So I figured I'd try some praying of my own. I prayed my parents would stop fighting."

Jeff pried loose a stone that stuck up through the surface of the snow and tossed it toward the lake, where it hit the ice with a hollow *thunk*, then skittered away across the blue-white surface toward the dark, open water. "Yeah? So what happened?"

"Nothing. That's the point. *Nothing* happened. So what good is praying?"

"But Nikki, you told me yourself God answered your prayer for help, when your parents were trying to make you have the abortion."

"Oh, sure. Some help. He kept the clinic from doing the abortion, and then look what happened. I'm the one that had to live through the rest of the pregnancy, and that wasn't easy. Giving up Evan wasn't exactly my idea of an answer to prayer."

"But Nikki, God doesn't say He'll make it so we never get hurt or have to go through anything tough. You're talking like He's some kind of . . . genie. Like He's just there to get us out of trouble." Jeff glanced sideways at her, checking her response. "A lot of times, when I do something wrong, I still have to take the consequences of what I did. I know He forgives me, but that doesn't just make everything bad in my life go away, you know?"

"No, I don't know. Look how my parents acted. That wasn't my fault. They're just both so wrapped up in their own lives that they don't even care about me. I don't even have a *family* anymore. Was that supposed to be some kind of answer to prayer?"

"Didn't you even hear from them when you were in the hospital?"

"Are you kidding?" The thought of her mother's unopened letter in her dresser drawer flashed through Nikki's mind, but she pushed it away. "Who needs them, anyway? I wouldn't talk to them even if they did call."

"But Nik! There must have been something that made them react that way. I mean, don't you wonder sometimes what—?"

"No! I *know* what made them do what they did, at least with my dad. He hasn't thought of anything but himself and his job in years, so when it came down to choosing between me and getting to be a judge, I didn't stand a chance. With my mother, who knows? I've never understood why she does anything."

"Nik, don't you think you'll have to work through some of this with them sometime? Otherwise, the anger's gonna kill you."

Nikki kicked at a drift, and snow and ice flew in all directions. "I don't think you're listening to me, Jeff Allen. They walked out on me when I needed them the most, and I *hate* them! Do you hear me?"

Jeff walked quietly alongside her, knowing she didn't really expect an answer. Their boots broke through the snow with a crunching sound that filled the silence.

"Anyway," Nikki added after a few minutes, her voice low, "even if there really is a God, He wouldn't be interested in me."

"Why would you say that?"

"Oh, Jeff, come off it. Look how I screwed everything up. How many high school juniors do you know who've already had a baby? And will you tell me how we always end up talking about this kind of stuff? You know, just once I wish we could have a conversation like we used to. One that isn't about . . . about everything that's happened this year."

Jeff caught her hand again as she slithered down another slick rock. But this time he didn't let go. He pulled her around to face him, and she squinted against the bright sky as she looked up into his eyes.

"That's part of the reason I came up here." He hesitated, then plunged on when she didn't answer. "To see if you're gonna make it."

"I'll make it," she said cautiously, but inside she could feel herself go as still as the ice they stood on. *Can't you see I don't want to talk about it? I want to forget, even if it's just for a little while.*

"You sure?"

Nikki pulled her gloved hand away from his and started out alone. "How would I know, Jeff? Sometimes I'm not sure if anything'll ever be okay again." She walked as fast as she could, but he matched her stride easily. "I try not to think about it, but it's always there. That was my child. Part of me. My body, my heart. And he's gone." Her voice quavered on the last word.

"But he's—"

Nikki turned on him. "Don't you dare say 'he's so much better off'! If one more person says that to me, I swear I'll scream!"

Jeff put both hands up as though to hold her off. "I wasn't, I wasn't, honest!"

They threaded their way carefully through a narrow strip between boulders at the mouth of the pier. Then Jeff spoke again.

"I'm sorry, Nik. I didn't know it was still so bad for you."

"*Still* so bad? *Still?* Oh, sure, it's been a whole month, so I should be over it by now, right?"

"No, that's not—"

"Your own father told me I'd think about this baby and worry about it the rest of my life. Don't you remember? That day we told him I was pregnant and he was telling me about adoption?"

Jeff nodded, and Nikki went on. "Well, what he didn't tell me was that I would love the baby like this. Love him, care about him, wonder how he's doing almost all the time. And—" she stared out across the broad expanse of white and her voice grew soft "—miss him. That I'd miss him more than I could have dreamed." Suddenly, she straightened up. "You know what I think, Jeff?"

"What?"

"I think that lasagna's probably ready."

❧ *Eight* ❧

NIKKI CUPPED HER HANDS AROUND the heavy pottery mug and drank the last of her tea. From where she sat, curled up in the corner of the living room couch, she could easily watch Gram and Grandpa on the loveseat, their eyes intent on images of the Serengeti Plain that flashed across the television screen. They could never resist a documentary about wildlife, and "Nature" on public TV was their favorite Sunday night program.

It was not quite as easy to see Jeff, who was stretched out comfortably in the recliner to her left, unless she turned her head. And she had no intention of doing that, since she'd been avoiding his eyes as much as possible ever since they talked on the beach earlier that day.

I wish Jeff would mind his own business, Nikki thought, looking straight ahead. *He's always trying to tell me how to live my life, what I ought to do about my family, about the baby, even about God.* Her anger at him had been growing throughout the afternoon and evening, even though another part of her—the part that thought rationally and calmly, and seemed to be getting smaller and smaller lately—kept telling her she was being totally unfair. *That*, in turn, made her even angrier at Jeff.

So when Chad rang the doorbell halfway through "Nature," Nikki found herself making more of a fuss over him than she normally would have. She led him around Gallie, who was standing in the way, barking and wagging his tail at the same time, as he always did with strangers. In the living room, she introduced Chad to Jeff and her grandparents. She stood close enough to his side to smell the leather of his jacket.

"Sit down, Chad. You're welcome to join us." Grandpa motioned toward the empty side of the couch. "It's just a wildlife program, but it's better than those 'Calamity of the Week' movies on the networks."

Chad sized up the situation right away and slid into what Nikki thought of as his ultra-respectful mode. "No, thank you, sir. I've . . . ah . . . I've already seen this one, I think. Actually, I'd rather take Nikki out if it's all right with you, just down to Rosie's. Sir."

Gram and Grandpa looked at each other, then back at Chad.

"I don't see any problem with that," Grandpa answered, glancing in Jeff's direction. "But I guess it's up to Nikki to say whether or not she wants to go."

Nikki motioned Chad back out into the hall, and as they passed the recliner, she could see the red patches high up on Jeff's cheekbones, the ones he always got when he was upset. Once they passed through the living room doorway, Chad put his arm around her shoulders and said, "So, sweet lips, where do we party tonight?"

Nikki had just opened her mouth to tell him not to act crazy when Jeff's voice cut in. "I thought you were just taking her down to Rosie's?"

Nikki whirled around and saw he had followed them to the hall, and she looked back and forth from his face to Chad's as they stared at each other. Over Jeff's shoulder, Nikki could see her grandparents wrapped up in their program again, unaware of what was going on. Jeff took a deliberate step forward and stuck his hands in his pockets.

"I hear the roads are kind of icy," he said.

Chad made a small, derisive sound with his lips. "The roads are fine. Besides, we're just gonna go work on my lines." His lips formed themselves into a definite smirk. "There's nothing I like better than rehearsing with Nikki. Know what I mean?" His eyes slid from Nikki's hair down to her feet and back up, very slowly.

"Just a minute," Jeff said. The red patches on his cheeks were nearly purple now, and he stepped across the hall till he was nearly toe to toe with Chad. "I don't believe Nikki wants to go anywhere tonight, at least not with you." Then his nose wrinkled as though he smelled something bad, and he leaned closer to Chad and sniffed.

Nikki could feel her own cheeks burning, both at Chad for acting so foolish and at Jeff for trying to interfere in her life again. She hesitated for a moment, imagining what would happen after her grandparents went upstairs to bed if she stayed here. *I'll probably get another one of Jeff's sermons about how I should live my life,* she thought, *and I don't think I can stand any more of those.*

She opened the coat closet and grabbed her gray down coat off a hanger, then turned to Chad. "So let's get going," she said.

Chad tried to open the front door but found his path blocked by Gallie, who was waiting eagerly for a chance to get outside in the snow. "Would you just get out of the way?" Chad said. He pushed the dog aside with his foot, then stepped out onto the front porch.

Jeff glanced back over his shoulder at the living room and lowered his voice so only Nikki could hear.

"Nik, where'd you find this loser?" he hissed at her. "You can't go out with him. He's been drinking!"

She had never seen him look so furious.

"Oh, can't I?" she shot back. "Listen, I'm sick and tired of you telling me what I should and shouldn't do. What gives you any right to do that?"

Jeff drew back as if she had slapped him, and Nikki cringed inside at the look on his face. But she couldn't seem to stop. "Just let me make my own decisions, would you *please?*"

Then she called over his shoulder to Gram and Grandpa, "See you later. I won't be late," and hurried to the car where Chad sat, drumming his hands impatiently on the steering wheel.

The last thing she saw as they drove away was Jeff standing at the front window watching them, his shoulders hunched over.

"Probably praying," she muttered to herself, and Chad said, "What's that, babe?"

"Never mind."

Chad reached out and pulled her close. "You're not in a very good mood. How about if I cheer you up? It's too cold to stop the car anywhere, but I know a few places where we could go. . . ." He leaned over and rubbed his cheek against the top of her hair, then kissed her cheek as he drove. And all of a sudden, she knew with a hollow, sinking feeling in the pit of her stomach that Jeff had been right about the drinking, because she could smell it, too.

Nikki looked out at the road, which was shining under the streetlights. The bright sun had melted the snow during the afternoon, then the cold night air had frozen it into a glistening layer of ice. *Gram and Grandpa would never have let me come if they'd known it was like this*, she thought.

She pulled away a little and tried to speak calmly. "Chad? I'm not sure this is such a good idea. I mean, with the ice and all. Why don't we go back and work on your lines at my house?"

"With loverboy checking every move I make? No thanks." He turned the corner a little too fast and the back end of the LeSabre slid toward the center of the road. Nikki gasped, and Chad laughed as he pulled it back into the right lane.

"You know what's wrong with you, Nik? You're so uptight you just don't know how to have fun. Like the other night at the concert. Everybody was hanging loose, and you just stood there all frozen and stiff." He gunned the engine and hit the brakes, and the LeSabre spun all the way around in the middle of the empty intersection.

"You've been drinking, haven't you?" she yelled, holding on to the dashboard with both hands.

"Oh, come on, Nik, I'm just having a little fun. There isn't another car in sight. This isn't exactly the big city, you know."

He took his hands off the wheel long enough to beat out a quick rhythm on the black vinyl, then in a final flourish, he slapped his hands together as though he held a cymbal.

"You're nuts," she cried. "You really *have* been drinking!"

"Okay, okay, Sherlock. So I found a little booze Dad thought he hid really well. Big deal. I didn't drink that much. Calm down, and I'll take you to Rosie's." He leaned toward her and spoke in the deep, theatrical voice he used whenever he tried to make her laugh. "I'll drink *black coffee!* That should help me sober up and go straight." He switched back to his usual voice. "At least, that's what they always give the guys in the movies who get soused."

Chad had eased up on the gas enough by then that Nikki had stopped shaking. She turned on him. "You've got more brains than this, Chad. Why on earth would you drink and then get behind the wheel?"

Chad laughed at her, one side of his mouth turned up in the

same smirk he had shown to Jeff, and nosed the LeSabre into Rosie's parking lot. "Look, if it's good enough for my old man, it's good enough for me. He hardly even makes an effort to hide his empties anymore. I think he's finally figured out that I'm old enough to know what he's doing. Especially when he falls asleep with his head in a plate of spaghetti." His voice dropped suddenly, as though he'd forgotten she was in the car.

Angry as Nikki was, she still couldn't miss the pain in his voice. "He did that?" she asked.

Chad jerked around to face her, and he pressed both lips together in a thin, tight line. "Kind of hard for you to imagine, isn't it, with your lawyer dad and all? Well, my old man used to be pretty classy, too. But all it takes is one phone call from my mom, and he's down the tubes."

"But you can't let that make you—"

Chad brought both hands down on the steering wheel with a thud. "Don't tell me what I can do!" He swore softly under his breath as he turned to stare out the window at the nearly-deserted parking lot. "She calls up and acts like she still has some kind of right to run my life." His voice took on a singsong timbre, and his head wagged back and forth. "'Chad, how's your school work? Chad, how's the play coming? Chad, how's your social life?'"

He swore again, and his words picked up volume. "So if she's so interested in my life, what's she doing in Colorado shacking up with that guy?" His voice went back to the singsong. "'Be careful when you drive, dear, and take good care of yourself. I can't tell you how much I miss you.' Then she pulls the same number on my dad, and he grabs the nearest thing with alcohol in it and starts guzzling." Chad's hands tightened on the steering wheel for a second, then he took a long, deep breath and released them. He reached across Nikki, pushed open her door and gave her a lopsided smile. "After you, ma'am."

Rosie's was empty except for the waitress, who didn't look any too happy about having customers this close to closing. She was wiping tables when Chad and Nikki walked in, and when she saw them, she tossed her rag toward the sink. It fell just shy of the counter and slid to the floor. The waitress shrugged, then pried her pad and pencil from her pocket and followed them to a table in the corner.

"Just bring me coffee," Chad said. Then he added, *"black coffee,"* drawing the words out and looking pointedly in Nikki's direction. She was relieved to see he was back to his usual self again, and she ordered fries so she could keep him at the restaurant as long as possible.

After the waitress arrived with their order, Nikki asked, "So, Chad, where's the script?"

As Chad looked at her over his mug, Nikki wanted to tell him what she was really feeling, what she really thought about people who drove when they'd been drinking. But in the face of his broad smile, with the white-blond hair falling down across his forehead, she couldn't seem to do it. Instead, hating herself for being so afraid to rock the boat, so unable to tell guys what she really thought, she found herself talking as though everything was back to normal.

"You said you needed to go over your lines, remember?" she prodded him.

Chad set his mug on the table, and a little of the black liquid sloshed over onto the gray formica. "It's out in the car. I guess I don't really feel like saying a lot of lines right now."

Nikki squirted ketchup over her fries from a red plastic bottle that had more caked on the outside than there was inside. The ketchup was so thin it dribbled down between the fries and onto her plate, and she wondered if Rosie was watering it down these days.

"Well, okay. We don't have to work, I guess," she told him. "Sounds like you've had a lousy day anyway."

"Don't worry about it, Nikki. It's my problem."

Not when you drive other people around drunk, it isn't, she wanted to say, but she didn't know where to start. So she said the first thing that came into her head. "Maybe you're going to have to accept what your mother did—"

Chad banged his cup down this time, and a whole wave of coffee joined the first little puddle on the tabletop, so Nikki went on as fast as she could, trying to make him understand. "I don't mean that what she did is *right*, you know? I just mean that, for your own sake, you may have to just . . . just . . . let it go. And get on with life."

Chad stared at her for a second, his eyes blazing. "That's a crock, Nikki, and you know it. How many people do you know who can just let something like that go. Huh?"

But Nikki could hardly hear him, her own words were so loud in her ears. *Just let it go?* a little voice in her head echoed. She thought about her mother's letter and how it still lay in the dresser drawer, unopened. *You're not just a hypocrite, you're world class,* the little voice said, *giving other people advice about forgiving.*

Suddenly, she just wanted to be home, alone, where she could think. "Chad, let's go. I'm tired," she told him.

In the parking lot, she tried to get him to let her drive, but he only laughed.

"Relax, Nik! I drank all my coffee, remember?"

He backed the LeSabre over the curb when he turned it around in the parking lot, and he hardly even seemed to notice. Nikki was tense most of the way home, expecting trouble. When they rounded the corner onto her grandparents' block, she finally let out a long sigh, relieved that they'd made it safely.

But she had sighed too soon.

At first, she didn't even realize there was a problem. And by the time she did, it was too late to do anything about it.

Gallie was playing in front of the mailbox, in the middle of the street. He'd never had to worry about cars, since the street dead-ended in the dune just beyond the Nobles's house. He was on his back now, rolling in the fresh snow, his paws flopping in that crazy way he had. Then he heard the noise of the car and seemed to sense something was wrong. His eyes, even upside down as he lay on his back, looked like a frightened deer's in the headlights. Nikki watched him helplessly as he scrambled to get his big, furry body upright and tried to run, but his hind legs kept slipping out from under him on the icy street.

There was plenty of room for Chad to go around him. It wasn't until she heard him yell, way too late, "There's a stupid dog in the middle of the road!" that she knew he hadn't seen Gallie in time.

"Chad, look out! Stop! *STOP!*" she screamed at the top of her lungs. But she felt the dull thud of the impact and knew that all the black coffee at Rosie's hadn't been enough.

❧ *Nine* ❧

WHEN NIKKI GOT UP THE NEXT MORNING, the house exuded a listening kind of silence, as though waiting for sounds of her grandparents or Gallie to fill its rooms.

She made her way to the kitchen, drank some orange juice from the cardboard container in the refrigerator, and read the note her grandfather had stuck onto the refrigerator door with a bronze magnet shaped like a teapot.

> Good morning, Nik,
>
> We left early for Gram's appt. at the hospital in Grand Rapids and we didn't want to wake you. The vet had to put a pin in Gallie's leg last night. He thinks it'll be basically healed in six weeks or so. He says the leg will probably never be completely straight again, but Gallie should be able to get around on it. They'll have to keep him at the vet's for a few days.

Nikki leaned against the refrigerator and closed her eyes,

trying not to think about what Gallie must be feeling. Instead, the picture of Grandpa and Jeff laying the big, golden-furred dog gently in the backseat of the car flashed through her mind, along with the picture of Gram's face, stricken and white, as she insisted on struggling into the car seat beside Gallie, cradling his head in her lap. Nikki opened her eyes quickly and read the rest of the note.

> We'll be home by seven or so. If your grandmother feels well enough, I think I'll take her out for dinner—it'll be hard for her to come home to the house without Gallie. See you then.
>   Love, Gpa

Nikki started to take another drink of juice, but her stomach turned. She pushed shut the cardboard spout of the container, set it back on the refrigerator shelf, and walked into the dining room.

She could see through the bay window that the sky was a solid, uninterrupted white, so that the snow-covered ground and the sky melded into one another with no horizon. And out of that featureless white backdrop, tiny hard crystals of snow were falling here and there.

The whole thing was my fault, she thought. *Gallie would never have gotten hurt if I hadn't been so pigheaded about going out with Chad. And it was all because I was so mad at Jeff, when all he was doing was trying to help.* Nikki hung her head, overwhelmed with remorse. Were mistakes always this easy to figure out the day after you made them? *Poor Gallie. How awful for him, and for Gram and Grandpa. And it's all my fault.*

She turned her back on the bleak picture outside the window and looked around the dining room. *I haven't exactly kept up my part of the housekeeping bargain lately either,* she thought. The great oak corner hutch was covered with dust, and the shiny hardwood floor under the table needed sweeping badly.

Through the arched doorway, she could see into the living room, where yesterday's paper lay strewn around. The cups that Gram, Grandpa, and Jeff had set down in such a hurry when they heard Nikki screaming outside were still sitting on the end tables, hot chocolate dried to a brownish froth around their edges.

She walked into the living room, rubbed her sock-clad toes over the claw feet on the sofa table to remove the dust, then picked up the newspapers. She stacked the sections in a ragged pile on the needle-point hassock, then sighed and sank down on top of the sports page, her head in her hands, remembering last night.

When she'd jumped from the seat of Chad's LeSabre and skidded across the ice to where Gallie lay in the road, the dog's moist brown eyes had held only love. Even in his pain, Gallie's furry muzzle rose an inch or so off the ice, and he made a valiant effort to lick her hands.

Chad, for once, had been at a loss for something to say. Even the words "I'm sorry" seemed to escape him. He stood rigid, his arms wrapped around himself, leaning against the fender of the car as Grandpa and Jeff ran out of the house and into the street, their first concern for Nikki and Chad.

In the bright white headlights of the LeSabre, which had spun a complete U-turn when Chad slammed on the brakes, Nikki had watched Grandpa as he knelt beside the dog, his wrinkled hands moving cautiously over Gallie's limbs. When his thick fingers probed Gallie's right hind leg, the dog's furry head jerked off the ice, and he gave an involuntary growl. Then he dropped his head immediately and whimpered as though to apologize, his feathery tail thumping weakly against the ice.

By that time, Chad's usual self-possession was back in place.

"I'm terribly sorry, sir," he told her grandfather. "I . . . I tried to stop and just totally lost control on the sheer ice. I'm just so sorry. I don't know what to say."

Listening to him, Nikki fumed inside. Either the coffee had finally taken effect, or the shock of hitting Gallie had sobered up Chad completely. No one except Nikki and Chad—and of course, Jeff—would ever guess the real reason Gallie had been hit. When her grandparents and Jeff left for the vet's, she had turned the full force of her anger on Chad.

"How could you *possibly* have hit him?" she yelled, gulping in great breaths of air that seemed to turned to ice in her throat and lungs. "I could see him plain as day when we were way back in front of the Allens', and you didn't even *try* to stop for another three or four seconds. Didn't you even *care?*"

Chad sucked in his bottom lip and chewed at it for a second. Then his chin came up a few inches, and he stared back into Nikki's angry eyes. "You're wrong, Nikki. I put on the brakes as soon as I saw him. It was the ice—I couldn't stop."

"You couldn't stop because you didn't try soon enough, and you didn't try soon enough because you'd been drinking!"

"So sue me." Chad shrugged and reached out to take her arm. "C'mon, Nik, give me a break. You know I didn't mean to hit him. Haven't you ever driven on ice?"

"I wouldn't ever be stupid enough to drive when I was drunk, whether there was ice or not! You don't have any idea how much Gallie means to Gram and Grandpa. When Gram had her stroke last summer, Gallie wouldn't even leave the house until she came out of the coma. And since Gram's been home, he almost never leaves her side except to go for a walk with Grandpa."

She'd ranted on and on, trying to explain how special, how important Gallie was, and then somehow Chad had his arms around her and she was crying against his leather jacket, and it wasn't his problem anymore—it was hers. And *she* was apologizing for bawling all over *him*.

Now, sitting on the living room couch surveying the mess around her, she shook her head in amazement. *What is it with Chad, anyway? He can worm his way out of anything.* She pulled a tissue from the pocket of her robe and rubbed it back and forth absently across the top of the coffee table until the dust was gone. *If only I hadn't tried to prove to Jeff that he couldn't tell me what to do, none of this would have happened.*

The night had gotten even worse after Chad left and she'd gone upstairs to bed. Wild dreams had plagued her sleep, dreams of screeching brakes and accidents. And then it all flowed back into the old nightmare about Evan, only this time with her mother included. It had been 3:00 in the morning when she wrote it all out in another letter to Evan and close to dawn when she finally got back to sleep.

Nikki gathered her tousled hair back with both hands and thought guiltily about Jeff. He had driven all this way just to spend time with her, no matter what he'd said about the house, and all she'd done was fight with him.

But every time she was with him these days, the talk always turned to God.

She turned and glanced around the room. Anything to get her thoughts off Jeff. *I ought to vacuum and pick up before Gram and Grandpa get back.* Maybe that way, she could make amends, at least in part, for all the trouble she'd caused. If she really got moving, she could even get a batch of brownies baked. Gram particularly loved brownies with walnuts, and Nikki was anxious to do something special that would let her grandmother know how very sorry she was.

She thought about calling Jeff and apologizing, and even picked up the phone, then hung it up again, telling herself he was probably sleeping in after his late-night trip to the vet. She got a rag and the furniture polish and started to dust the right way. Keeping busy was better than thinking about facing Jeff.

Nikki was just taking the brownies out of the oven when Keesha called two hours later to see if they could finish sorting through the things they'd found in the attic. In a few minutes, Keesha's brother dropped her off, and when she opened the door, Nikki was surprised to see that snow was falling once again.

"You think it'll ever stop?" Nikki asked, squinting up at the gray sky. The girls went inside and headed together up the two flights of steps. Keesha had to haul herself up by holding on to the stair railings and pulling.

"Keesha, if you get any bigger, this will definitely be the last time you make it up these stairs," Nikki said.

"Girl, if I get any bigger, I'll explode!" Keesha laughed, her breathing loud and labored.

Nikki laughed, too, from where she stood in the attic doorway, then stretched out her hand to give Keesha an extra pull. "It's like you got bigger just since Saturday!"

"Nothing 'like' about it," Keesha puffed, as she reached the last step. "I gained two more pounds this weekend." She glanced down at her leopard-patterned T-shirt, the brown spots on the black background stretched completely out of shape by her swollen belly. "Well, *one* of us did, anyway. Bring on the Mounds bars!" She stood still for a minute, surveying the piles of clothes and shoes left from Saturday. "We sure made a mess, didn't we?"

Nikki knelt beside the last trunk she had opened on Saturday and began looking through the jewelry in the top tray. "I know we can use some of these things," she told Keesha. "Look at this heart-shaped locket. I think it'll be just right for Jen to wear with that navy-blue dress."

She lifted out the tray and searched through the rest of the trunk but found no clothes. Instead, there were two spiral-bound notebooks, their covers decorated all over with hearts and names of couples drawn in blue ink. There was a stuffed tiger with an ear torn halfway off and one eye missing, and a shoebox full of postcards and notes. Underneath these was a certificate, yellowed around the edges, from Howellsville High School. "For Participation in *Brigadoon*," it read. "Rachel Suzanne Nobles."

My mother, Nikki thought, staring at the paper she held. It seemed impossible to imagine her mother as a teenager who collected notes from other girls and saved a stuffed animal that was in such bad condition she probably wouldn't even allow it in her perfectly-decorated house in Ohio.

At the bottom of the trunk lay a thick, brown book with soft, dog-eared corners. Nikki flipped it open and scanned the neat blue letters, written in rounded, childish handwriting on the faded blue lines of the paper.

Keesha was folding dresses in a box, mumbling, "Keaton's gonna kill us. We don't have nearly enough stuff for this play." She used the side of the trunk to pull herself up off the floor.

But Nikki hardly noticed what she said. She had flipped the brown journal open near the back, and her eye fell on the words: "June 10. I will never, never, <u>never</u> trust anybody again, as long as I live. It was all lies, all these years, just lies." The line under the word *never* was so deep it made an indentation Nikki could feel with her finger through the next several pages. She glanced inside the front cover, but there was nothing to indicate what year it was written or whose it was.

It has to be my mother's, though. Everything else in this trunk is hers. My mother's—so why do I even care what's in it? I don't want anything to do with her anymore—not with her letter in the dresser drawer in my room, not with her diary, not with whatever silly problem she was having way back then. But she couldn't help being curious.

She frowned and looked at the next entry.

"Nikki . . ."

"They don't know it," she read, "but I called him. I finally got his name out of Arleta and . . ."

"*Nikki . . .*"

". . . he said I could meet him next week, so I'm going to take the bus into . . ."

"*NIKKI!*"

Nikki jerked her head up. Keesha's eyes were open so wide that white showed all the way around the pupils. Her mouth was open, too, her breath coming in quick, shallow gasps.

"What's the matter, Keesha? What's wrong?"

Keesha looked down at her legs, spread slightly apart in the black stretch pants.

"Keesha!" Nikki demanded. "What is the matter with you?"

Keesha looked back up. "I'm all . . . I'm all *wet*."

"No! You can't be, Keesha. You're not due for another two weeks!"

Keesha heaved a great sigh. "You think you're telling me something I don't already *know*? Where's your phone? I need to call the doctor."

Nikki snapped the journal shut and dropped it back in the trunk. "Can you make it back down the stairs?"

Keesha gave her a disgusted look. "'Course I can. Just let's get going."

By the time they reached the second floor hall, Keesha was completely out of breath. Nikki led her into Gram and Grandpa's bedroom and pushed her gently down on the edge of the bed, then ran for the hall phone. Keesha sat for a second, then struggled back up to her feet.

"You have something I can sit on? I'm getting this bed all wet."

"Here," Nikki said, thrusting the phone at Keesha. "I'll get some towels. Do you know his number? Do you need the phone book? It's downstairs, but I can run down and . . ."

"Don't worry. I know it," Keesha said, her fingers shaking as she punched in the numbers.

Nikki grabbed two thick rose-colored towels from her grandparents' bathroom shelf and ran back to lay them on the white chenille bedspread, trying to keep the memories of her own labor from flooding back into her mind. She could remember all too well the waves of pain that had cramped her midsection with each contraction, pain that seemed to knot itself tighter and tighter as the hours dragged by.

Keesha sat on the towels gingerly, the phone propped between her shoulder and ear, patting her black pants to see how wet they were. "They put me on hold, wouldn't you know it. Hello?"

Nikki listened as Keesha explained three times, to three different people, what had happened, her exasperation growing with each repetition.

"They're *finally* gonna get the doctor," she told Nikki after the third repetition. Keesha told her story for the fourth time, then listened silently. After a few minutes, her face relaxed into a smile. "Oh, that's good. That's good. Yeah, we will. Okay, thanks." She hung up the phone. "I have to go to the hospital in Grand Rapids, Nikki. But Dr. Grover asked me if I'd had any labor pains yet, and when I told him no, he said not to go so fast we get in an accident or anything. He says the water broke, but as long as I don't go into labor right away, we'll have time to get there. Whew!"

Keesha sagged back against the bed pillows with relief but pushed herself upright quickly when Nikki asked, "Aren't you going to call your mother?"

Her face seemed to crumple. "Nikki, my mother went into Howellsville to see my grandmother. Grandma called early this morning and said her furnace wasn't working right, so Mama went right off to help her."

"What about your brother who dropped you off?"

"He was on his way to work—in Howellsville."

"Your sisters?" Nikki asked, with a sinking feeling.

"LaNae's gone to class—Howellsville College has school today—and Leilani's at work. The other two are in Detroit, visiting my aunt."

"Where does Leilani work?"

"Down beyond Columbia about 15 minutes, at that outlet mall. You know that one that just opened last fall?"

Nikki tried to think. Grand Rapids was 45 minutes to the east, and Howellsville and Columbia were half an hour in the other direction. To get anybody in Keesha's family to come home and pick up Keesha, then leave for Grand Rapids, would double their time to the hospital.

"So we'll get an ambulance." Nikki reached for the phone, but Keesha stopped her.

"Our insurance doesn't pay for ambulances."

"Hang on, Keesha." Nikki ran down the hall and jerked up the shade on her side bedroom window. The red Bronco was still there, in the driveway between her grandparents' house and the Allens'. Jeff hadn't left yet.

She started back down the hall for the phone, then stopped.

She thought of Jeff's face the night before, when he tried to warn her about Chad—and how he'd carefully avoided looking at her as he and Grandpa struggled to keep their footing on the icy road when they lifted Gallie's limp body into the car.

She hurried back to her grandparents' room. "I know what we'll do," she said, picking up the receiver. "We'll call Chad." She recoiled at the thought of getting back into the LeSabre beside him, but she dismissed the thought. *Don't be stupid, Nikki. He'll be fine by now. It's not like he's an alcoholic.*

"Great," Keesha moaned beside her. "The most gorgeous guy in town, and I get to ride with him looking like *this*. Do I get all the luck, or what?"

Nikki waved a hand to shush Keesha and counted the telephone rings. Finally, on the seventh one, a low voice answered.

"Hello?"

"Chad, is that you?"

"Nikki?"

"Yeah. Listen, Chad, I need some help."

"Hey, babe, I'm glad you're still speaking to me after last night. Just couldn't resist all this charm, right?"

"Chad, *listen*. Keesha's having her baby. She needs a ride into Grand Rapids."

There was a pause. "So where's her family?"

"They're gone, Chad. Her mother's in Howellsville and her sisters and brother are gone at . . . Listen, what's important here is that Keesha's got to get to the hospital and she doesn't have a way."

"Well, I hate to be the one to let you in on this, but that's why God made ambulances, you know?"

"Her insurance doesn't pay for an ambulance. All she needs is a friend to give her a ride."

"Yeah, well, that's cool, Nik. For somebody else, I mean, but not me. I wouldn't exactly call myself a friend of hers, you know what I mean?" Nikki could feel her face starting to burn. She opened her mouth to answer, but Chad continued. "Like, what if she has the kid in the car? On the side of the road, you know? I wouldn't have any idea what to do, that's for sure."

"What's he saying?" Keesha whispered. "Can't he take me?" And then, on the word *me*, her mouth dropped open and her eyes flew open wide the way they had in the attic when her water broke. Only this time, she grabbed at her middle, her hands clamped on either side of the leopard-spotted bulge.

"*Nikkiiii!*" she wailed.

"What? What now?"

"I think—" she breathed hard as she struggled to speak "—I think . . . this is a . . . contraction." She rocked back and forth on the bed, hugging her middle, then spoke again when she caught her breath. "Oh, man, Nikki, you mean there's gonna be more of those?"

Nikki didn't hesitate. She hung up on Chad, dialed Jeff's number, and within five minutes, the three of them were in the Bronco headed for Grand Rapids.

❧ Ten ❧

NIKKI THOUGHT THE RIDE to the hospital would never end. The white flakes, which had been falling only sporadically when Jeff first backed the Bronco out of the driveway, thickened to a nearly blinding curtain before they had driven 15 minutes. Wind off the lake lashed icy, wet snow against everything in its path, creating an ominous frosting that obscured traffic lights and exit signs.

At first, the uneasiness between Nikki and Jeff caused an awkward silence. But now, with the Bronco crawling along at 20 miles an hour and Jeff's attention riveted on the barely visible road ahead, the urgency of getting Keesha to the hospital on time united them.

Nikki glanced in his direction, at the Chicago Cubs hat he wore backward and the dark, stubbly hair along the line of his jaw. He saw her watching him and rubbed his hand over his chin.

"Sorry," he apologized, grinning at her. "I didn't see any reason to shave. I was just about to leave, and I didn't think I'd see anybody before I went."

Nikki figured that hating to shave was a family trait, since Dr. Allen grew a full, dark beard every summer at the lake and was always talking about razor-free vacations.

By the time they reached the main highway, Keesha was working hard to hold back the tears that came with each contraction. Jeff glanced into the rearview mirror and caught sight of her face where she sat in the backseat.

He slipped his maroon letter jacket off his shoulders and handed it to Nikki. He wore a faded Banana Republic shirt underneath, one she remembered from the summer and their walks on the dunes.

"Fold this up like a pillow, would you, Nik?" He looked back into the mirror. "Keesha? Try to stretch out on the seat and see if it hurts less that way. You can use my jacket for a pillow, okay?"

Keesha lay down with small grunting sounds, and Nikki unfastened her seatbelt and squeezed between the seats to help her. She tried to plump Jeff's jacket into a serviceable pillow, then tugged off her own down coat for Keesha to use as a cover.

"Hey, are you gonna make it?" Nikki whispered, her face close to her friend's.

Keesha looked up, and Nikki saw that tears were mixed with the sweat on her face. "I don't think it's supposed to hurt this way, Nik. This isn't like what they told us in childbirth class." She sighed and the tears came faster. "It's punishment, Nikki."

"What?" Nikki frowned, holding on to the seat to keep her balance as she crouched in the narrow space beside Keesha. Then she gave a short laugh and tried to make light of the girl's words. "I bet every woman in the middle of labor says that."

But Keesha shook her head. "No, I'm serious. God's punishing me. He knew I wanted this baby, and now it's coming early and it's gonna die. . . ." Her voice trailed off in a sob, and she gritted her teeth and closed her eyes tight against another contraction.

She looks like a little girl, Nikki thought, scanning Keesha's full cheeks and rounded chin. *A little girl with a woman's job in front of her.*

Nikki smoothed her friend's hair gently, laying some of the tiny tangled braids straight. "Oh, come on, Keesha. Don't talk crazy. Why would God be punishing you, anyway?"

Tears slid down Keesha's face faster now, following one another in an unbroken stream, and Nikki fumbled in the pocket of her coat, which now covered Keesha, for a tissue. She wiped carefully at the tears and perspiration, but Keesha turned her face into Jeff's coat and shook her head.

"'Cause of what I did, two years ago. . . . " Her voice was muffled by the coat, indistinct and broken by hiccups, but Nikki sucked in her breath when she made out the words. "I had . . . an abortion. I couldn't tell you the truth, the other day in your room. I could never have an abortion again. *Never.* But now this baby's . . . going to die, too."

Suddenly, in her memory, Nikki was back on the beach with her grandfather, on that foggy morning the previous summer when she felt as though the struggle over her own pregnancy would tear her apart.

She could still hear his words. *"Some women carry the effects of an abortion all their lives. What looks like the simplest answer now may cause you the most trouble in the long run."*

And she remembered how Evan—even though she hadn't thought of him by name way back then—had looked on the ultrasound, how he turned and kicked and made his way into her heart simply by the intensity with which he lived his own life there inside her.

Nikki rubbed Keesha's back gently, patting the space between her shoulder blades that still shook with teary hiccups, because she had no words to say. She tried desperately to think of something appropriate, but it was Jeff who managed that.

"Lord," he began to pray into the silence in the truck, "all three of us—no, all *four* of us—need Your help here. Me, because I need to get us to the hospital safe and in time. Keesha, because she's feeling like You can't love her or forgive her after what she did. Help her to see the truth about that, and please let this baby be okay.

"And Nikki—" twin taillights appeared in the snow ahead of them, and Jeff tapped the brakes lightly several times before he went on "—well, You know all the stuff she's struggling with. Please help her hear what You're trying to say to her." His "amen" was drowned out by Keesha's loud moan as another contraction knotted itself around her middle.

Once Nikki had realized Jeff was actually praying, and out loud, she'd closed her eyes and prepared to be embarrassed. Praying was meant to be a late-at-night, alone-in-your-room activity as far as she could see. But his words had a different effect than she'd expected. She felt instead a kind of envy growing inside her—envy that Jeff knew someone he could turn to for help.

When Keesha's contraction ended, she heaved a long sigh, then rolled slowly from her side to her back and lay contemplating the gray velvety fabric of the ceiling panel over her head. After a few seconds, she said, "Amen. Thanks, Jeff." A slow smile curved itself onto her tear-stained face. "Mama always prays like that around our house."

"You got through to her, right?" Jeff asked.

"Yeah, I called her right after Nikki called you," Keesha answered. "And . . . Jeff?"

"Um-hm?"

"You really think God forgives people for stuff like this?"

Keesha's eyes stared straight up at the ceiling again, and Nikki felt like an intruder on a very private conversation.

"That's what He says," Jeff said quietly. He steered the Bronco cautiously around a semi that had jackknifed on the highway. "He forgave me, Keesha."

When at last they reached the emergency room, there were a few minutes of total confusion as workers milled around, trying to get information, deciding what should be done. Jeff and Nikki stood on the sidelines, watching as Keesha was finally loaded onto a stretcher and covered with heated blankets.

"Can't I go with her?" Nikki asked the nurse, trying to calm the panic she saw in Keesha's dark eyes as the orderly arrived to wheel her away. "I could stay with her at least till her mother gets here. . . ."

The orderly, the nurse with her clipboard, and the emergency room doctor palpating Keesha's abdomen all shook their heads in a definite *no*.

"There might be some problems," the doctor answered, his voice low so that only Nikki and Jeff could hear. "Things may get a little rough before it's all over. There's a waiting room up on the fifth floor, in maternity. We'll catch you there later."

All Nikki could do was wave, helplessly, as the stretcher was rolled away and the double wooden doors swung shut behind it, squeaking back and forth on their hinges in the now-empty hall.

It was all just like she'd been remembering for a month—the antiseptic odor, the constant paging over the intercom—and she shuddered, trying to shut off the memories before they got started.

She turned to look at Jeff, and with Keesha taken care of, the awkwardness was there between them again.

He was watching her, his dark-blue eyes steady on hers.

"Jeff?"

His eyebrows lifted in answer.

"I'm sorry about last night. You were right. Chad *was* drinking and I, well, I should never have . . ."

Jeff pushed back his hat and scratched the side of his head. "Yeah, well, don't worry about it. Carly's always telling me I ought to quit bossing people around so much, and she's probably right. C'mon, let's go find your grandparents."

He turned now and started down the hall, and she followed him with the uncomfortable feeling that her actions the night before may have put more distance between them than she'd intended.

Jeff stayed long enough to have a sandwich in the hospital cafeteria with Nikki and her grandparents—and to hear that Keesha's baby girl, delivered by emergency C-section, would be fine. Then he called the state police and found out the snow had stopped to the south of town and the highway was now passable.

"I better get going," he told the three of them. "I called Mom and Dad and explained what happened, but I think they'd feel better if I'm home before it gets too dark." He thrust his arms into the sleeves of his jacket. "Will you tell Keesha I said congratulations?" he asked Nikki.

"Sure. I know she'll want to call you herself and thank you for everything anyway."

They walked to the elevator together, and Jeff put out his hand to press the button for the first floor, then hesitated.

"Listen, Nik. I don't know why it's so hard to talk to people about things like this, but it is," Jeff said, the red patches on his cheeks visible again. "So I'm just going to say it straight out, okay?

I'm afraid you don't really believe what I said to Keesha in the car—about God forgiving people. Think about it, would you?"

Then he punched the button, the door slid open, and he was gone.

It was another hour before Nikki could see Keesha. Her friend looked exhausted, and her braids were jumbled together, splayed out in all directions across the crisp, clean white of the pillowcase. But she was smiling and her brown eyes sparkled when she saw Nikki tiptoe toward her bedside.

"C'mon in. It's all right, I'm awake. Have you seen her?" When Nikki nodded, Keesha went on excitedly. "Isn't she *gorgeous?* And not a thing wrong with her, Nikki. Not one single thing! But that's thanks to you and Jeff, because she was turned all wrong and Dr. Grover said she never would have been born normally. That's why it hurt so much."

Then she looked a little abashed. "He also said the baby wasn't two weeks early like I thought and that I probably had the wrong date." She rolled her eyes. "I told him I had the wrong date, all right—only not the kind he meant! That guy was the wrong date from the very first time we ever went out."

Nikki laughed, relieved that Keesha felt well enough to joke around again.

"I watched the nurses give her a bath and get a footprint and all that," Nikki said, "but they should be done by now."

"Well, they better get her in here soon," Keesha said, "'cause I can't wait to hold her."

"What about you? Are you okay?" Nikki asked, her forehead wrinkled with concern. "I mean, didn't the operation hurt?"

Keesha just laughed. "Nope. All I felt was some tugging and

pulling, you know? Like a giant wrestling match in my middle. But not pain. I think they gave me the same thing you had, where you don't feel anything from the waist down. 'Course, when the block wears off, it may be a different story.

"I nearly dropped dead from fright, though," Keesha continued. "When they told me they were gonna have to do a C-section, I said, 'Get out of here! No way you're gonna cut me practically in half.' But when they held the baby up and showed me, oh, man, Nikki, I couldn't believe it." She shook her head slowly back and forth on the pillow, the dark braids tumbling this way and that, and Nikki saw there were tears in her eyes.

The heavy wooden door swung open and stopped with a soft thud against the wall. Keesha's great dark eyes widened, and Nikki turned in her chair toward the doorway. A nurse was pushing a clear plastic bassinet in from the hall. When she'd positioned it next to the bed, the nurse reached inside confidently and scooped the baby up into her arms, then lowered her toward Keesha, who had to stay flat on her back for the next few hours, until the medicine wore off.

"Here you go, Mama!" the nurse said, smiling.

Keesha and Nikki both stared at the tiny bundle, wrapped tightly in a blue-and-pink receiving blanket and capped with a pink knit hat. Keesha reached out slowly, cautiously, and gathered the baby into her arms. A broad smile spread across her face as she watched the baby's dark eyes open, saw the little arms flail and the miniature fingers and hands move haltingly, in small jerking starts, as though the baby was unfamiliar with the operating instructions. Keesha pressed her forefinger carefully into the pink palm, and the tiny fingers closed around it instantly.

The baby opened her mouth in a huge yawn. A shudder ran through her whole body, then she gave a little mewing sound and closed her eyes. "She's asleep, Nik," Keesha whispered. "Just like that."

Nikki was dimly aware that a feeling of pain had been growing somewhere in the region of her chest for the last few moments. She watched as Keesha laid her cheek against the baby's and rubbed it softly up and down, then kissed the fuzzy pink hat and the black hair that showed around it, then each of the wrinkled fingers that curled around her own.

Nikki had been able to hold the pain at bay while they worried about Keesha, and while Jeff paced the halls with her, and while she ate a late lunch with him and her grandparents. But now it swelled inside her, like a thick sludge behind her tongue—pain that could not be forced down, though she swallowed over and over, afraid it would choke her.

It was four weeks and three days ago, right in this hospital, right on this floor. Only it was me then, waiting for the nurse to bring my baby. The smells, the sounds, the sights—everything worked together to bring back the scene she'd been trying so hard to shut out of her mind.

She closed her eyes and saw him again. Evan, *her* Evan, his dark-blue, long-lashed eyes peering out at her from beneath the blue knit cap. He had the same miniature hands as Keesha's baby, hands that had wrapped themselves with amazing strength around her forefinger and hung on for dear life.

And she'd pried those fingers loose herself. Broken that clutch. Handed him off to strangers.

The longing to feel that creamy soft skin and breathe in the scent of his warm, yeasty baby smell overwhelmed her.

"Keesha? Please, can I hold her?" she said. She put all her effort into keeping her voice steady, but even then, she wasn't entirely successful.

But Keesha didn't even notice. She looked up, surprised, and

Nikki knew she'd been off in a world of her own. Keesha nodded silently, and Nikki leaned over the bed and slid her arms beneath the sleeping baby.

Nikki held her close against her chest, as though the small slumbering form could salve the feeling that ached there. The baby's soft puckered lips moved in sucking motions for a moment, then fell into a relaxed line, the bottom lip shaking slightly each time the baby's sweet breath passed over it.

Nikki didn't realize she was crying until a tear dropped onto the soft nap of the receiving blanket, and she shrugged one shoulder up to wipe the tears off her cheek.

Keesha turned her head away, toward the hall, and fingered the stiff, starched edge of the white hospital bedspread awkwardly. "Mom should be here any minute."

Nikki didn't answer.

Keesha tried again. "Hope she makes it okay with all this snow." Then she turned her head back abruptly. "How'd you do it, Nik? Give your baby up, I mean?" She reached out for the child, and Nikki laid the warm bundle gently back in her arms. Keesha's dark eyes looked up into Nikki's. "Maybe you could still get him back." Then she dropped her head against the baby's and murmured, "I know I could never give her up. Not in a million years."

When Mrs. Riley finally arrived, Nikki said her good-byes to the accompaniment of thank-you hugs from both Keesha and her mother, then went to find her grandparents with a sigh of relief.

Gram and Grandpa had given up their idea of going out for dinner because of the weather and decided to start for Rosendale immediately. As her grandfather steered the car carefully over the newly-plowed expressway, Nikki curled herself into a tight ball in the corner of the backseat.

Keesha had no idea how her words had cut. *She can't,* Nikki thought. *And she'll never have to. She gets to take her baby home, gets to rock it and hold it and kiss it whenever she wants.*

❧ Eleven ❧

BY THE TIME NIKKI FINISHED all 45 sit-ups and 10 "cats," got herself into jeans and a green sweater, and walked through the front doors of the school on Tuesday morning, she'd figured out exactly what she wanted to say to Chad.

I think it was pretty low that you wouldn't even help Keesha get to the hospital yesterday. I mean, the girl was in labor. Can you understand that? But you wouldn't help. Oh, no. You were too busy, or too tired, or too something.

Maybe she'd throw in a little about Gallie, too. Like how his leg would never be completely straight again, thanks to Chad's driving.

Nikki had plenty to say, that was for sure. But when she finally rounded the corner by the locker room door and found Chad, she didn't say one word of it, because Bryce Putnam was already there, and he appeared to be doing all the talking.

She watched, openmouthed, as Bryce slammed Chad flat against one of the lockers and held him there, one huge hand twisting Chad's shirt tightly into a straitjacket.

Though Bryce was in both her English and Spanish classes,

she hardly knew him because he rarely deigned to talk to anyone but other seniors. But she was aware, along with the rest of the school, that he always seemed to be in a fight with someone.

Now Bryce leaned forward, his face almost touching Chad's. "We had a *deal*, remember?" he said. "You used the tickets, so you get the paper here—*on time*. And let me warn you. I don't know what you New York boys do when somebody doesn't keep up their end of a deal, but I'll tell you what we do here." He shoved Chad backward again, and a shudder ran through the gray metal lockers. "We make 'em sorry—real, real sorry. Understand?"

Bryce jerked his hand away so suddenly that Chad slumped forward like a rag doll, then caught himself halfway to the floor.

Nikki turned and fled back around the corner before either Chad or Bryce saw her. She detoured through the cafeteria and choir room and was sitting in English class with her book open to the page Mr. Keaton was reading in *Beowulf* by the time Chad strolled calmly into the room.

What tickets was Bryce talking about? she wondered. *It had to be the tickets to the Black Tail Spin concert. Then what paper is he talking about? What did Chad promise him to get those tickets?*

"So glad you could be with us, Mr. Davies," Mr. Keaton said, glancing across the top of his half-round reading glasses.

Don't start in on him right now, Nikki pleaded, suddenly protective at the memory of Chad splayed against the locker, at the thought of how hard he must be working to hide his feelings. She worried that Chad's temper would spill over onto the unsuspecting teacher, but Chad, as always, surprised her once again.

"Sorry, Mr. Keaton. The car wouldn't start. I had to jump it." Chad slid into his seat just as he always did, then reached back and squeezed Nikki's knee twice to say hello.

"**S**o where were you *really?*" she demanded as they left class together after the bell rang.

Chad looked at her with a thin wrinkle of annoyance between his eyes. "Jumping the LeSabre, like I said."

For a second, she toyed with the idea of telling him what she'd seen before class, but before she could say a word, Mr. Keaton called her from the front of the room.

"Nicole? Nicole!"

She turned in the doorway to face him.

"I hear Keesha had her baby. And that she had a C-section."

Nikki nodded, touched by his concern, and started to describe their trip to the hospital the day before, but Mr. Keaton cut in.

"That's great," he said, glancing at his watch. "Listen, I have a faculty meeting I have to run to. I just want to make sure you're taking care of props, since Keesha will be out of commission for several weeks. I need whatever you can bring me by tomorrow."

Nikki sighed. She'd never gotten back to the piles of clothes, shoes, and papers in the attic that she and Keesha had left unfinished. "Sure, Mr. Keaton. By tomorrow," she repeated, thinking how long it would take to get the attic put back together. And the journal . . . She'd fallen asleep thinking about it the night before, too tired after everything that had happened with Keesha to climb up the stairs and retrieve it.

She turned quickly back toward Chad, but he was already gone. She could pick out the back of his blue shirt in the crowd halfway down the hall, and she thought in frustration, *What was Bryce talking about, anyway?*

During Spanish class, when the principal knocked on the door and motioned Ms. Valdez out into the hall, Nikki tried to plan how she'd get everything done that night.

Besides all the homework she had to finish, there was Gram's therapy to help with. The physical therapist in Grand Rapids had given her a whole new set of exercises for her arm and leg. And then there was the time Nikki was supposed to spend singing with Gram. And dinner and dishes and the vacuuming she hadn't quite finished on Monday.

And now, on top of all that, I'm supposed to get Mr. Keaton this stuff from the attic. There was no way she'd ever get it all done in one night. And to make matters worse, it was hard to even keep her eyes open. The dream about Evan had come back last night, over and over, until she lay staring wide-eyed into the darkness, trying to prop her eyes open to hold off sleep.

Seeing Keesha's baby or being back at the hospital—or both—must have triggered it. Three times she'd woken up, sweating, with her long, flannel nightshirt tangled and twisted around her. Once, all the bedclothes, including the pillows, were on the floor.

And for the first time, writing about it hadn't helped calm her down at all. She had stopped after three pages, stared at what she'd written, then torn the pages savagely from the pad, crumpled them to a tight ball, and dumped them into the wastebasket.

I don't want to write to Evan! I want to talk to him. I want to feel him in my arms and hear him cry and laugh and . . . I want to do all those things Keesha will get to do. I just want him back.

And then, curled up on the window seat in the middle of the night, she'd cried so long and so hard that her eyes still felt grainy, as though sand had wedged itself underneath her eyelids and scratched the fragile tissues every time she blinked.

Nikki folded her arms on her desk and laid her head against

them. *That's what's really wrong,* she thought. *Not all this stuff I have to do. It's Evan.*

As she struggled to sort out her thoughts, Nikki became gradually aware that Ms. Valdez was back in the room and was speaking in Spanish. *"Espero que no te molestara tu descanso!"*

Nikki automatically began to decipher the words in her mind.

"I—hope—I'm—not—disturbing—your—nap!" On the last word, Nikki jerked her head upright and found Ms. Valdez looking directly at her. From the seat behind her, she could hear Bryce's snorting laughter.

As it turned out, Nikki had a lot more time than she'd expected when she arrived home. Aunt Marta's white Taurus was parked in the driveway, and Marta and Gram had already worked their way through all the new exercises and several songs.

Nikki tried hard not to show the relief she felt at having Aunt Marta there. She knew it wasn't the kind of thing you would ever say out loud—such as, "Gram, you're taking up too much of my life"—but just the same, it was a relief to have it off her shoulders for a day. And just because she felt guilty at being so relieved, she found herself saying, "Well, what about dinner, then? I could at least get something started. . . ."

Aunt Marta looked up from the piano, her hair pulled back and twisted as usual in a long teakwood clip so that the curly ends erupted above the back of her head like some obscure volcano. "Don't worry, Nikki, everything's under control. I'm doing dinner tonight, so you and Dad are on vacation."

"Where is Grandpa, anyway?"

Marta vamped a few melodramatic measures on the piano, then laughed. "The mad professor's in his study, scribbling about bugs or bacteria or some other riveting subject that'll keep his readers—all three of them—clinging to the edge of their seats."

"Marta!" Gram laughed. "You should talk."

"What?" Marta looked up in mock astonishment. "You're lumping *my* book on polyphonic texture and chromaticism in Baroque music with Dad's bug articles? I never was appreciated around this house." She grinned and played a short introduction to "Amazing Grace" and said, "Come on, Mom. Two more verses to go."

"So what are you making for dinner?" Nikki asked before the singing started up again.

"German spaghetti," Marta said.

German spaghetti, a name that had set the whole family groaning when they first heard Marta describe her new specialty, had turned out to be delicious. Now Marta fixed it regularly, whenever she was in town long enough to cook.

Nikki went to the kitchen and grabbed a diet soda from the refrigerator and an old sweatshirt from the coat tree. On her way through the front hall, she knocked on the study door.

"Hi, Grandpa! Just wanted to see how you're doing."

He glanced up from his computer keyboard and smiled absently. She went to stand behind him and, setting her drink and sweatshirt on the desk, began to massage his shoulders gently.

"Looks like you're working pretty hard here," she said.

He frowned briefly, then shook his head back and forth and went on typing. "Not too hard. I'll be out for dinner, okay?"

She smiled to herself as she climbed the steps to the attic. Grandpa was so delighted to be able to research and write again that he could hardly stay out of the study long enough to eat.

The attic was cool and silent after all the noise downstairs. Nikki pulled on the fleecy black sweatshirt over her green sweater, jerked the soft, frayed string that hung from the lightbulb, glancing around at the mess she and Keesha had left. If she worked really fast, for about an hour, she could probably pick out all the things she thought Mr. Keaton could use *and* get everything else put back before dinner.

By the time the dusty daylight from the small attic window faded to darkness, Nikki had filled the box Keesha started with clothes, shoes, and jewelry. The rest she repacked as neatly as she could. As she started to close the lid on the trunk that held her mother's things, her curiosity got the best of her. She reached inside and pulled out the brown journal, then sat, Indian-style, on the floor under the bare bulb that dangled from the ceiling.

She could hear faint sounds from Aunt Marta and Gram in the kitchen two floors below, and the smell of onions and garlic seeping up the stairs told her dinner was well underway. But as soon as she found the June 10th entry and reread it, Nikki was totally wrapped up in what was written there, trying to figure out what the words meant.

"I will never, never, <u>never</u> trust anybody again, as long as I live," Nikki read again, noticing once more how deeply indented was the heavy blue line under the final *never*. "It was all lies, all these years, just lies."

What could have made her mother that angry? But as soon as she thought it, Nikki gave a short laugh.

Of course, the real question is, what doesn't *make my mother angry?* she thought. For as long as Nikki could remember, it had been one of the facts of her life—Mrs. Sheridan's anger, lying just below the surface, ready to erupt at the slightest provocation.

She's just like Chad, she thought suddenly. *He's smooth and sophisticated and always acts so cool, but just underneath that, he's like a hand grenade waiting to explode.*

At least with Chad, she understood why.

Nikki stopped and turned to the previous page of the journal, looking for a clue, but the entry for June 9 dealt with nothing more than swimming lessons and a trip to Howellsville with "Mom and Daddy" to buy a new swimsuit.

Nikki stared at the writing and tried to imagine Mrs. Sheridan as a girl who could call her parents "Mom and Daddy," but she drew a blank. It was much easier to connect the mother she knew with the angry person who had written the later entry. She turned the page.

"June 15. They don't know it, but I called him. I finally got his name out of Arleta and he said I could meet him next week, so I'm going to take the bus into Grand Rapids and meet him at the Denny's downtown."

Who could she be meeting? A guy? But that didn't fit in with the anger of the earlier entry.

There was another entry, dated June 23, and it made no sense at all to Nikki. "He said I should leave him alone, that he never wanted to see me again."

Nikki started to leaf through the rest of the cloth-bound book, but there was a shuffling, bumping sound at the bottom of the stairs, and she called out, "Who's there?"

In answer, the top of Marta's head, with even more of her gray-streaked dark hair worked loose from its haphazard arrangement than usual, rose through the floor cut-out that formed the door to the attic. As she watched, Nikki thought gray like that would have sent her own mother flying in panic to her hairdresser, who kept Mrs. Sheridan's every carefully-colored strand of hair in perfect order. When Marta wiggled the rest of herself through the doorway and safely onto the attic floor, she brushed the dust off her hands and turned slowly in a full circle, her glance taking in the huge room that came to a point in the ceiling rafters.

"*Whew!* I haven't been up here in years. And I definitely don't remember those stairs being straight up and down!"

"You left Gram alone?" Nikki asked.

Marta glanced at her for a second, then continued surveying the room. "She's fine, Nikki. She's watching the sauce for me."

"The sauce? But she doesn't cook anymore," Nikki protested.

"She does now," Marta said. "In fact, there's a whole lot of things she'd like to start doing again, if you and Dad would quit coddling her. She says she has to fight you two to do just about anything these days."

"She got on me about that when Jeff was here," Nikki said. "About not letting her talk."

"That's the best possible sign—for her to fight back this way, I mean. She wouldn't do it if she wasn't getting better."

Nikki watched as her aunt inspected a shelf piled with old gilt-edged plates and saucers.

"I forgot all about these." Marta gave a short laugh. "We used to use them when I was younger than you are right now. I guess I finally broke so many we had to get a new set. Your grandpa was always warning me that would happen if I wasn't more careful when I did the dishes."

Marta switched back to her original subject without a pause. "I think you should know, Nikki, that it's not unusual to get a little tired of taking care of other people now and then."

Nikki squirmed. "But I'm not . . ."

Marta swiveled on one sneaker-clad foot and fixed Nikki with a challenging look, her eyebrows high above the top of her glasses.

Nikki hung her head, and Marta was quick to speak. "Nik, it's okay. You've done a great job with Gram. Everybody needs a break now and then." She poked around in the box Nikki had set aside for Mr. Keaton. "Is this the stuff you found for the play?"

Nikki nodded.

"Looks good. I can help you get it downstairs if you want." Marta peered back down the stairs through the floor opening and grinned. "Actually, I think the easiest thing to do would be to just throw it all down from here, and then pick it up when we get there!"

"Aunt Marta!"

"Just kidding, just kidding," Marta said hastily. "Between the two of us, we'll get it down there somehow." She saw Nikki watching her skeptically. "No throwing. I promise." She sat down on the lid of a sturdy-looking trunk and looked at her niece.

"I see you found your mother's journal."

Nikki nodded.

"Did you read it?"

"I just started."

Marta watched her for moment, as though she was about to say something, then changed her mind. "So, Mom tells me you're into emergency deliveries these days. You and Jeff."

Nikki described Monday's ride into Grand Rapids with Keesha in labor, and Marta followed every word, leaning forward with her hands between her knees, her eyes narrowed.

When Nikki finished, Marta shook her head back and forth and sighed. "You and Jeff are lucky—make that *very* lucky—you didn't end up delivering a baby somewhere between here and Grand Rapids." She pushed her glasses back into place on the bridge of her nose. "So tell me, were you okay? About being back at the hospital, I mean?"

Nikki hesitated. She had always admired the way Aunt Marta could casually air a topic that everyone else was knocking themselves out to avoid, but now she wondered if there was such a thing as being too direct.

"What do you mean?" she stalled.

"It had to be hard on you to go back there, Nikki. It's only been a month."

"And four days," Nikki corrected her automatically.

Marta leaned across the space between them to pat her knee, but Nikki didn't respond.

"You want to talk about it?" Marta asked.

At first, Nikki just stared down at her brown suede shoes, at the wavery, milk-white line around the bottom where snow and salt from the road had wet them, then dried. And as she stared, she swallowed over and over, until she could force down the hard lump in her throat.

"It was just . . . I mean, I was glad when Keesha was all right," she said slowly, trying to make some order of the feelings that whirled around inside of her. "And I'm glad for her, that she gets to keep her baby. I just . . . I guess I just wished . . . that *my* mother was more like Keesha's, and wanted me to keep the baby, wanted to help with him."

"You really miss him, then?" Marta asked.

Nikki nodded, staring at the shoes again and the wavery line that now seemed to swim in her tears. *Miss* was such an inadequate word for the storm of emotions she felt whenever she remembered Evan, with his round little face, his dark, wet hair that curled just a little at the ends, and the warm, biscuity smell of his skin. Or when she watched Keesha kiss and cuddle her new baby daughter.

"I miss him so much, I don't think I can go through with this," she answered, startling herself.

Marta frowned. "Can't go through with what?"

"I think maybe I was wrong to give the baby up."

Marta's eyebrows came together in a dark line over her glasses, but she remained silent, peering at her niece as she spoke.

"I didn't know how much it would *hurt*," Nikki defended her words. "I didn't even know there *were* feelings like this until he was born."

She felt naked somehow, in the light of Marta's scrutiny, and she drew her knees up to her chest and buried her face against them.

"I can't even think straight anymore," she said, her words muffled against the denim of her jeans. "I can't think, I can't sleep—and I keep having this stupid nightmare. . . ."

"About the baby, you mean? Oh, Nikki," Marta said, her voice low and sorrowing. "How long?"

"Ever since I came home from the hospital," Nikki answered.

"Well, then," Marta said, and Nikki could hear that her aunt, famous in the family for solving problems, was mentally rolling up her sleeves for action. "We have to do something to help you get through this. How can we get this situation resolved?" she asked, more to herself than anyone else.

Nikki lifted her head. "You can help me get him back," she answered, and hearing herself say the words solidified the thought in her mind.

"Nikki!" Marta cried. "You can't do that. You signed papers in the hospital, didn't you?"

"Yes, but they're not binding," Nikki answered. "I don't go before the judge for another week and a half—until Friday the 12th. Up until then, I can still change my mind. . . ."

"Nikki, think what you're saying!" Marta demanded. "You wanted your baby to have two parents, two *grown-up* parents, remember? And a stable home."

"I *know* what I said then." Nikki glared at her. "But this is what I'm saying now. I want him back."

"Excuse me, but you're not thinking straight here." Marta pushed her hair back off her forehead and blew out a long, tense sigh. "Your responsibility is to do what's best for the baby,

remember? If I'm not mistaken, that's why you made this decision in the first place. And now, because your decision hurts, you're
ready to forget all that. Exactly what kind of life would you be offer-
ing him, Nikki? You'd have to go to work to support yourself and
you haven't even finished school. And who would take care of the
baby while you worked? Who would take care of *you*?"

Nikki looked up as Marta's voice broke. "I'm 17, Aunt Marta.
Nobody needs to take care of me." She could sense the rightness of
everything her aunt had said, but something in her made her fight
back, made her words sharper than she'd intended. "Besides, it's
my decision, not yours."

Marta sighed. "That's true, in one sense. But it's best to get
input from your family, too—"

Nikki pushed herself up off the floor and dropped the journal
into the box on top of the clothes and shoes. "Oh, sure. Some
family! Like my father, you mean? Whose only input was to schedule an abortion without even asking me? Or maybe you mean my
mother, who was worried that a *grandchild* around the house might
ruin her perfect image. Is that the family you mean?"

"Nikki, stop it!" Marta pleaded. "You miss the baby. Of course
you do. That's only normal. But I don't think that's the real problem here, at least not all of it. There are some other things you have
to straighten out first."

"Oh, right, and now I suppose you're gonna tell me what my
real problem is!"

"You're angry, Nikki, and you don't know how to handle it.
Both Mom and Dad told me that ever since the baby was born,
your anger's been growing and growing. Your grandpa said that
when your mother's letter came last week, he was afraid you were
going to explode."

"Great. So now you all sit around and discuss me behind my

back, right?" Nikki demanded.

Marta took her hands away from under her chin and sat up perfectly straight. "Yes, we do. You're absolutely right. And we do it because we care about you, Nik, so stop acting like a child. You're right about my sister—Rachel will never win the mother-of-the-year award. And what she and David did was wrong, and I'm not trying to justify that or make any excuses for them. But Nikki, you can't carry this anger at them around forever. It's keeping you from thinking straight. It's almost as bad as the anger you feel at yourself."

Nikki could feel her cheeks flush. "At *myself*? What are you talking about?" she shouted. "It's my parents I'm angry at! If they were normal parents, I'd probably still have my baby. Look at Keesha's mother. Keesha gets to keep her baby, because she has a mother who cares about her."

"I don't think for a minute that getting the baby back is the real answer," Marta said. "I think you just want to stop the pain. And listen to me, Nikki. There are other ways to do that, ways that won't work overnight, but that make a lot more sense. You need to deal with your own anger. You need to read that letter from your mother and give her a chance to have her say. And there're some things you need to say back to her, too, Nikki. You can't just let that anger keep simmering inside you like this. You have to find some closure to this whole thing, a way to let go—"

"Would you just leave me alone about *closure* and *letting go*? I thought you were a musician, not a psychologist! I don't need some amateur shrink to analyze me, okay? I know what my problem is—my parents."

But Marta was shaking her head slowly, definitely. "That's not the only problem. Look, Nikki, I know that Rachel's writing upset you—"

"It didn't *upset* me. It made me really *angry*, okay?" Nikki crossed her arms over her chest. "I mean, come on, Aunt Marta! Wouldn't it upset you? After everything she's done, now she just decides to come waltzing back into my life, right? Well, no thank you!"

"I'm not saying there's any excuse, but sometimes, if you listen, you can start to see why people do things."

"I don't *care* why she did it. Doesn't anybody understand that? And just stop with all the analyzing and advice, would you please? All I need is to get my baby back!" Nikki headed for the steps. "I'm going downstairs."

Marta's shoulders sagged, and she got to her feet slowly. "Well, at least let me help you with the box. Since it certainly seems like I haven't helped with anything else," she added, and Nikki could hear the misery in her voice.

Something inside her wanted to accept Marta's help, to make things right between them again, but her anger wouldn't let her. "No thanks. I don't need your help!"

Nikki jerked and slid the bulky container across the rough wood floor to the first step, then heaved it with difficulty into her arms and staggered down the stairs.

❧ Twelve ❧

MARTA'S GERMAN SPAGHETTI DINNER, cooked perfectly and served with a bright-green spinach salad and fresh, hot bread, tasted like sawdust in Nikki's mouth. Marta picked at the strands of pasta on her plate, winding them around and around her fork but seldom putting the fork to her mouth.

Gram and Grandpa looked back and forth between Nikki and Marta with worried looks and worked hard at keeping some small talk going. It wasn't until Arleta stopped by in the middle of dinner with a box from the bakery that the conversation picked up.

"I THOUGHT YOU MIGHT LIKE SOME CRANBERRY MUFFINS," Arleta said as she trailed behind Marta, who had let her in the kitchen door. Nikki could see immediately that teal was the color of the day—teal shirt, teal jacket, teal earrings.

"THEY'RE FROM VAN KAMPEN'S BAKERY, AND YOU KNOW HOW GOOD THEIR STUFF IS! I STOPPED ON MY WAY HOME FROM THE LIBRARY. OH, YOU'RE EATING! I GOT YOU RIGHT IN THE MIDDLE OF DINNER."

Nikki rolled her eyes and poked at the orange sections nestled against the green spinach leaves on her salad plate. *Big surprise!* she thought. *Like we'd be doing something else this time of day.*

She looked around the bright room with its shade drawn against the chill winter darkness, at the fragrant red sauce over the spaghetti, and at the fresh flowers Marta had brought for the table. Grandpa pulled up an extra chair for Arleta, and Marta rushed another place setting in from the kitchen. Nikki felt so isolated from them all by the hot anger inside her that she might as well have been standing outside in the dark, ankle-deep in the snow, peering at them through the steamed-over glass.

Even though she would never admit it to herself, she knew her anger was out of all proportion to Marta's words in the attic. Gram's and Grandpa's worried, trying-hard-to-understand looks were making it even worse. And now, on top of everything else, Arleta's constant, deafening chatter threatened to push her past all endurance.

Marta was just about to serve dessert when the phone rang. Arleta was still talking, naturally, about spumoni for dessert and some study that proved people in Italy lived an average of seven years longer than anyone else because of all that olive oil they used.

As Nikki jumped up to get the phone, she could hear Arleta's voice behind her as she walked to the kitchen.

"MUST BE A YOUNG GENTLEMAN. THAT'S THE ONLY THING THAT MAKES GIRLS MOVE THAT FAST THESE DAYS. IS HE NICE? WHAT'S HIS NAME?"

Nikki gritted her teeth and picked up the receiver.

"Hey!" Chad's voice greeted her, as though the incidents with Gallie and Keesha and Bryce had never even happened. "How'd you like to come watch rehearsal?"

Nikki had pretty much decided over the weekend that going out with Chad any more was out of the question. But she could hear Arleta's voice from the dining room—*actually, the whole town can probably hear Arleta's voice,* she thought—and Marta was due to leave first thing in the morning. *If I stick around here tonight, she'll be in my room till all hours, wanting to get this thing settled.* Marta could never rest until everything was "settled."

She lowered her voice. "Have you had anything to drink? At *all?*" she pressed him.

Chad's voice sounded hurt. "C'mon, Nik! A guy makes one mistake and you think he's some kind of wino. You're so incredibly open-minded—that's what I love most about you. And anyway, like I told you, I wasn't *drunk* the other night. That dog of yours was on glare ice. Nobody could've stopped a car on that stuff. And to answer your question, no, I haven't had anything to drink. At *all,*" he mimicked her voice. "Unless you count the Coke I had at dinner. So are you gonna come or not?"

"NO, ROGER," Arleta was saying, "I'M SURE IT WAS SEVEN YEARS LONGER THEY LIVED—I READ IT IN *HEALTH UPDATE* JUST LAST WEEK."

Nikki groaned. *There's no way I can stay here. I could take my Spanish homework with me and work on it while I watch practice.*

"Well, I'll go if I can talk my grandparents into it," she said finally. "They don't get real excited at the thought of you driving on ice, you know? If I can go, will you help me take in the clothes I found in the attic?"

"Sure. And listen, just tell your grandparents the roads are perfectly clear. No ice at all. I'll be by in half an hour."

It was difficult for Nikki to make any connection between the Chad she'd seen flattened against the lockers that morning, his face contorted as he struggled in Bryce's grasp, and the Chad she watched now, rehearsing his lines as Tom Wingfield in *The Glass Menagerie*. From the moment he walked onstage, Nikki forgot all about the open Spanish book in her lap.

Chad knows exactly how to carry himself, she thought, watching his blond, hands-in-his-pockets casualness as he strolled across the bare wood floorboards. She couldn't help comparing him with Jeff, who would be lacing his fingers together and cracking all his knuckles at once, the way he did whenever he got nervous.

And his timing is perfect. When Chad stepped to the front of the stage, he waited a fraction of a second longer than anyone else would have, until every eye was on him. Only then did he launch into his narration.

"'Yes, I have tricks in my pocket, I have things up my sleeve,'" he began, and Nikki sat there trying to figure out exactly what it was about him—that something extra, that quality she couldn't pin down—that set him apart so clearly from Meg Coletti, who played the mother, and even Jennifer Van Kampen, the prettiest blond in school and daughter of the bakery Van Kampens, who had the role of Laura.

It isn't just the way he knows his lines either, she thought, although his delivery sounded professional in comparison to Meg, who was stumbling over a word in at least every other line.

"'Animals have sections in their stomachs which enable them to digest food,'" Meg recited emotionlessly, as though reading straight out of a biology textbook, "'without masti . . . mastic—' Mr. Keaton, I don't see why I can't just say *chew!*" She plopped her elbows down on the table in front of her and stared out into the tiers of seats at her disgruntled English teacher.

Mr. Keaton looked up from his script with a tight-lipped smile. "Because we don't change the author's words, Meg," he said in a singsong voice that a kindergarten teacher might use. "Remember?

Now try it again. The word is *mastication. Mas—ti—ca—tion*. Have you got that?"

Jennifer, on the other hand, looked as beautiful and fragile on stage as Nikki supposed the real Laura would have, and she apparently knew her lines perfectly. *But hardly anybody will ever know that*, Nikki thought, *since no one past the third row can hear a thing she's saying.*

Mr. Keaton controlled himself fairly well throughout the first scene, with only an occasional, "Louder, please." Then came an emphatic "*Louder, Jennifer, louder!*" But finally, halfway through the second scene, he decided to grapple with the issue head-on.

"'It was the lesser of two evils, Mother,'" Jennifer was saying in her normal dry, whispery voice. "I couldn't go back up. I—threw up—on the floor!'"

Mr. Keaton threw his script to the floor and strode onstage, left hand on his diaphragm, and planted himself in front of her. "It's got to come from here. Right *here*." He whacked himself in the region of his ribs. "You have to start projecting, Jennifer. *Projecting*. Or this play will go down—the—drain. Understand?"

Mr. Keaton whirled around and stood beside Meg's chair and faced the nearly-empty rows of seats. "'I couldn't go back up. I—threw up—on the floor!'" he proclaimed, and his voice rang through the room. He spun to face her. "Now, have you got that?"

Jennifer nodded, her eyes large and dark in her white face.

"Then *show* me!" he thundered, his voice filling the auditorium.

Jennifer took a deep breath, opened her mouth wide and squeaked.

Mr. Keaton's whole body stiffened, and the toes of his Adidas sneakers seemed to turn in even more than usual.

Nikki couldn't help laughing. *I wish Keesha could see this. I can just hear what she'd say.* "Whooaaa! Run for cover, Nik, he's about to self-destruct!"

Actually, Nikki thought suddenly, *what Jen really needs is a few lessons from Arleta,* and the idea made her chuckle.

She could just picture it. By the time Arleta finished with her, Jennifer would probably blow Mr. Keaton through the back wall of the auditorium: "'*I COULDN'T GO BACK UP! I—THREW UP—ON THE FLOOR!!*'"

Mr. Keaton was making absolutely sure Jen understood. "Make your voice come from here," he cried. "Right *here!*" He whacked his ribs once again with the flat of his hand, and Nikki winced.

Onstage, Chad was leaning against the painted fire-escape backdrop, his arms crossed in front of him. He caught Nikki's eye and winked at her, and she could see he was trying to keep from laughing, too.

But by the time Mr. Keaton got Jennifer projecting as far as the fifth row instead of the third, Nikki had lost interest. She was still trying to memorize the 15 new Spanish vocabulary words from the book in her lap, but thinking of Arleta had taken her thoughts back to things at home and the conversation in the attic that afternoon.

Marta, who was 10 years younger than Nikki's mother, had always been more than just an aunt to Nikki—she'd been a kind of combination big sister and friend. Nikki cringed at the thought of the biting words she'd flung at her aunt.

They'd had many conversations over the years, and Marta was always blunt, to-the-point, straightforward. But never harsh and mean, the way Nikki had been with her.

But that didn't stop me, oh no. "Would you just leave me alone about closure *and* letting go?" she could clearly hear herself shouting. "*I thought you were a musician, not a psychologist, and I don't need some amateur shrink to analyze me, okay? I know what my problem is—my parents."*

And just as clearly, she could see Marta shake her head and reply, *"That's not the real problem."*

By now, rehearsal was into scene III. Chad whirled to face Meg, his stage mother, and moved smoothly into his lines. "'I'm going to opium dens! Yes, opium dens, dens of vice and criminals' hang-outs, Mother. I've joined the Hogan gang, I'm a hired assassin, I carry a tommy-gun in a violin case!'"

In her seat, Nikki grinned at Chad's smooth insolence that added just the right touch to his lines. It was the attitude he was best at, one that seemed to come naturally to him, and he was able to control everyone in the room with his delivery.

It's because he doesn't just play a character. He actually becomes the character.

Watching with rapt attention, she realized that Chad was always in character, on stage and off, and she found herself wondering suddenly who the real Chad—underneath all the roles he played—really was.

At the end of the scene, Chad's voice changed, and Nikki came back to the present with a jolt. Chad was delivering his last line at Meg with such ferocity that he seemed to startle even himself.

He stood in front of her, legs wide apart, and stared down at her.

"'You'll go up, up on a broomstick, over Blue Mountain with 17 gentlemen callers!'" Then he bent over, slamming both hands down on the table, and shouted into Meg's face. "'You ugly— babbling old—*witch*. . . .'"

Nikki sat back against her chair, stunned by the violence in his voice, and realized she'd been holding her breath until he finished.

In the car, Chad waved away Nikki's words of praise.

"But you were," she repeated. "You were absolutely terrific. I had no idea you were that good."

Chad glanced over his right shoulder and started to back out of the school parking lot. "Thank you, thank you, ladies and gentlemen!" he intoned in his imitation of W. C. Fields. "And now, if you would be so kind, *please* hold your applause." He gave a wicked little laugh and returned to his normal voice. "Just throw money, honey."

Nikki relaxed in the face of his good humor. *This is so much better than sitting at home with Marta and all the rest of them.* If she put her mind to it, maybe she could pretend the conversation with Marta never even happened. *As a matter of fact, there's a lot of other things I'd like to pretend never happened, too, while I'm at it.*

"Listen, Nikki," Chad said as he steered the car toward Rosie's, "how'd you like to do another concert with me?"

"Black Tail Spin again?"

"Not this time. I got tickets for—" he did a quick drum roll on the steering wheel "—Alternative Nation." He braked at a stop sign and looked over to see her reaction.

"Alternative Nation! When?"

"Friday night. In Chicago. We'll have to drive about three hours to get there, but what's three hours between friends?" He reached across the seat and pulled her close to the side of his brown leather jacket. "Right?" He rubbed his chin gently across the top of her head, and the warm scent of his cologne seemed to fill the car.

We'll be almost to Jeff and Carly's if we drive that far, Nikki thought. And it would mean another whole night she wouldn't have to sit home alone, thinking. Or writing to Evan.

"You wanna go, Nikki?" Chad urged softly, his lips moving against her hair.

"Sure," she answered. "I'll go. I really like some of their stuff."

"Hey, you know that one they do—'Burn the World'? That is the coolest song." He swung the LeSabre into Rosie's parking lot and switched off the ignition. "Actually, from what I remember, the whole night's pretty cool. One big party, you know?"

A little tingle of doubt niggled at the back of Nikki's mind. She thought about Gallie at the vet's, his leg probably swathed in layers of plaster, and about her resolve not to date Chad anymore. *How would he drive three hours home, after a night that was "one big party"?*

Inside the restaurant, they talked over huge slices of banana cream pie. With her fork, Nikki fished out all the brown banana slices from the fluffy custard and piled them at the side of her plate.

"What are you doing?" Chad asked, his fork poised in midair.

"Getting all these gross brown bananas out of here. I never eat them."

Chad set his own fork back on his plate. "Well, excuse me for asking a stupid question, but why do you order banana cream pie, then?"

Nikki grinned at him. "I like the way it tastes, but the bananas always get dark and slimy." She held up a limp slice of fruit that was almost black. "See? Case in point."

When they discussed the play practice, Chad had only scorn for his co-actors. "Meg needs to take reading lessons, and Jennifer can't talk loud enough to hear herself. Now there's a cast for you." He shrugged. "Oh, well, who cares? It'll get me a great grade in Keaton's class, even if I don't do anything else in there all semester."

Nikki watched him chew, his mouth turned up on one side in his nearly permanent expression of disdain. "Do you always have an ulterior motive?" she asked.

Chad looked up in surprise. "Of course," he said easily. "Don't you?"

Nikki ignored his question. "You sounded really angry when you finished that last scene. You know, where you yelled at Meg?"

"Well, I was supposed to. I was acting a part."

"It sounded like a lot more than acting," Nikki said slowly.

"Whoa, Dr. Nicole! So now you're going to figure me out, huh?"

Nikki laughed uneasily and put a forkful of pie crust into her mouth.

"Well, you're too late, babe. My mother already sent me for counseling when she got ready to fly the coop. She wanted to make sure I *adjusted*, if you can believe that."

"Oh, yeah?"

"Hey, she got more than she bargained for, let me tell you. This counselor—it was back in New York City—this guy really had an attitude. He used to tell me, 'The only way to work through this is just to let your anger all out.' Kind of like that radio shrink we heard the other night. It made a lot of sense to me."

"So did you? Let it all out, I mean?"

"Doctor's orders, right? Not that it made any difference," he said, stabbing the crust into tiny pieces with his fork. He looked up at Nikki and laughed, and his laugh was a short, harsh sound in the air between them. "My mother never even listened to anything I said when she was winding up to leave. She still doesn't, even when she calls and tells me how much she misses me. She just sent me for counseling because she didn't know what else to do with her own guilt, but she was on her way out the door no matter what I said.

"Anyway," he continued, "I already told you, I don't want to talk about her. Why don't we turn the tables here and you tell me what was bothering you when I called tonight. You sounded like a guitar string ready to snap."

Nikki shook her head. "Just a . . . family talk, you know? With my Aunt Marta."

"Not a real pleasant one, huh?"

She shrugged. "Not exactly."

Chad pushed the blond hair back off his forehead with one hand. "You know, Nikki, you haven't been in the best of moods since Keesha had the baby yesterday."

"And just what is that supposed to mean?"

"Well now, let me look into my pocket-sized crystal ball and see if I can figure it out." Chad leaned back with his elbows on the arms of the chair, his fingertips together in front of him. "Number one, you practically spit nails every time the subject of parents comes up. Two, you're living with your grandparents and doing your junior year in a whole different state from where your parents live. Three, you never, ever talk about the fact that you just had a baby. I think, just maybe, I see a pattern developing here."

He hurried on. "Not to mention number four, which I already brought up. Ever since your friend Keesha had her baby yesterday, you've been moping around, wearing your heart on your sleeve. It doesn't take too many brains to figure out you're pretty steamed that she gets to keep her baby and you didn't. So, am I warm? Cold? Or right on target?" He reached across the table and speared two of her banana slices with his fork. "Besides, when are you gonna stop letting everybody push you around? Nobody can *make* you give up your baby, you know."

Stunned at the thought that her feelings were that transparent, Nikki tried to deflect the conversation. "Well, since you brought up Keesha, let me just say that you were a really big help yesterday."

Chad's face went suddenly sober. "Listen, yesterday was not the time to leave my dad to go chasing off in some snowstorm. Besides, it's not usually like the sitcoms, where every kid in the world gets born in 20 minutes. I figured you had plenty of time to call somebody else, and I was right, wasn't I?"

"They ended up doing an emergency C-section because the baby was turned wrong and wasn't getting enough oxygen. Both of them could have died."

He shrugged. "Yeah? Well, you didn't tell me all that when you called, now did you?"

"I just think you could have at least tried to help, that's all."

Chad leaned across the table. "Nikki. Yesterday was a year to the day since my mom left, and my dad pretty much lost it. Let's just say he wasn't even worrying about where to hide the bottles this time. He didn't even notice when he got to the bottom of one and started on another."

Nikki felt a twinge of pity, thinking of Chad spending that long, snowy day off of school taking care of his drunken father. At the same time, she was frightened that he'd go back to exposing her thoughts and feelings about the baby.

She pushed her chair back and folded her arms across her chest. "Why was Bryce so mad at you this morning? Down by the locker room?"

This time she had the satisfaction of seeing Chad look startled for a second, then he quickly masked his surprise.

"Bryce?" he laughed. "Ah, that was no big deal. Just a little misunderstanding."

"Oh, sure," Nikki said. "Some misunderstanding. I thought he was gonna kill you and stuff your body in the locker."

Chad's fair skin flushed across his cheekbones. "Get this, Nikki. Bryce is an idiot. I talked him into giving me those tickets for Black Tail Spin, and somehow he got the idea I was going to write his English paper for him."

"What do you mean, 'somehow he got the idea'? Did you tell him you would?"

Chad laughed. "Would I do that? The guy's got muscle where his brains should be, you know?" He pushed his chair back and stood up. "Come on, we better get going."

Once they reached the parking lot and got inside the car, Chad turned the key in the ignition, but didn't put the LeSabre in gear for a moment. Instead, he reached across the seat and pulled Nikki close to him, then tilted her chin up with one hand. But when he leaned down to kiss her, the face that filled her mind was T.J.'s. The memories of how she'd gone along with him the night she'd gotten pregnant, and of what had happened since, flooded her thoughts.

She twisted away from Chad so that his lips landed against her left ear.

"What's the matter with you?" Chad demanded.

"I just . . . I just don't want to, that's all." She slid back across to her own side of the seat. "Come on, you're the one who said we needed to go."

With one hand, Chad shifted the car into drive, and with the other, his fingers drummed a slow, steady meter on the steering wheel as he stared straight ahead.

"Well, I guess that pretty much lets me know where I stand," he said.

❧ *Thirteen* ❧

WHEN NIKKI STEPPED INSIDE the kitchen door, the first thing she noticed was the smell of popcorn that filled the air, almost masking the faint scent of wood smoke from the fireplace. She could hear voices from the living room—the deep bass of her grandfather's, along with the higher treble of Gram's and Aunt Marta's—though she could not make out their words.

She took a can of cold tomato juice from the refrigerator door and walked through the hall to the living room doorway. "Hi. I'm home, but if you don't mind, I'm going right upstairs. I still have some homework to finish."

Gram smiled and nodded, and Grandpa held out his bowl of popcorn. "Sure you don't want some of this?"

Nikki refused his offer and thanked him. She tried not to look directly at Aunt Marta, who she could see was watching her with a steady look from her seat on the brick hearth.

It took only 15 minutes to finish her Spanish assignment, then Nikki got ready for bed and switched off the light. With all the dreams about Evan interrupting her sleep lately, an early night wouldn't be a bad idea. But instead of drifting off, she tossed and turned, shifting positions every few minutes.

Thoughts of what Chad had said at Rosie's that evening filled her mind at first, then she replayed the argument with Aunt Marta word by word. After nearly an hour, she was more wide awake than ever, and she switched the light back on. The brown journal lay on her dresser, where she'd left it when she carried the box of clothes and shoes from the attic down to Chad's car earlier that evening.

She slipped her arms into her robe, picked up the journal and took it to the window seat. She backtracked and reread the last entry she'd looked at that afternoon. "He said I should leave him alone, that he never wanted to see me again."

The next entry was dated June 24. "So now I don't have any father at all. It turns out Daddy's not my real father, and the man who really is my father doesn't want anything to do with me. He has a family of his own, and when I met him at Denny's, he said his wife doesn't know anything about me and that if I ever called him again, I'd be in big trouble."

Then the journal entries stopped. Nikki searched back and forth through the pages that followed, but they were bare.

At first, she couldn't take in the meaning of what she'd read. The words were clear enough, but what they said seemed so impossible that she knew she must have misunderstood. She went back and read them again, slowly, just to make sure. Then guilt washed over her, guilt at reading something so private without permission. *But I didn't know, at first, that it would be anything like this. I thought it would just be about boys at school or something.*

And along with the guilt came an even stronger emotion—fear. She had to find out what her mother was talking about, because if Grandpa wasn't her real father, then what did that make

Nikki? And why hadn't she ever heard any of this before?

She thought back to what Arleta said in the kitchen when she was giving Gram the perm and how Gram's cup had dropped when she said it. Nikki had thought then that it was just a coincidence, but now she wasn't so sure.

Nikki sat holding the journal, staring at the words, wondering what to do next. *It's not like I can call Mother and ask what it all means, not when we haven't even spoken to each other since that day she and Dad left.* The only other thing she could think of was her mother's letter. She went to the dresser and pulled open the bottom drawer, searching under the summer clothes until she found it. She ripped it open and began to read the typewritten pages.

Dear Nicole,

After thinking things over for the last several months, I've decided that I at least owe you an explanation of what happened this past summer. And maybe of the past 17 years.

I'm sure you feel that I haven't been much of a mother to you. The truth is, when I was much younger than you, I decided that I would never have children, never hurt them the way I'd been hurt.

I know you think your grandparents are nearly perfect, but there's a lot more to their story than you've ever known. They grew up together—their families were close friends and went to the same church and such—and never looked at anyone else but each another. Until Grandpa went off to the Korean War, that is.

He'd been at Michigan State, studying biology and driving home every weekend to see your grandmother, who was still in high school. When he was drafted, they got engaged before he left and made all the kinds of plans engaged people do—how many kids and what kind of house, etc., etc.

But he was gone for two years, and during that time your gram won a music scholarship to U. of M. Two years is a long time when you're 17, as you know, Nicole, and there was another music student at the university that she saw and worked with every day.

Nikki had a sinking feeling as she read, as though she stood at the edge of a cliff, and once she looked over, nothing would ever be the same. But she had to know.

Gram's letters to Korea got farther and farther apart and then finally stopped, so your grandfather knew something was very wrong. When he got home, he went straight to her house. And found out she was pregnant. And alone. The music student had taken off the minute she told him she was going to have a baby.

Nikki read the last paragraph over four or five times before it finally sank in. Then she thought how Gram and Grandpa had invited her to come live with them last summer when she was pregnant, about how loving and understanding they'd been.

The way they tell it, Grandpa went off by himself for about a week, sick at heart, trying to figure out what to do. But in the end he decided that he loved Gram more than anything else. So he came back and told her he'd like to adopt the baby—me—as his, and he proposed all over again.

You know your grandfather. Once he decides something's over, he never mentions it again. And he and your grandmother have obviously made a wonderful marriage out of a really bad situation. They just neglected to do one simple thing—tell me. I know it wasn't the fashion back then to tell your children they were adopted, and your grandparents thought they were doing the right thing. But they were wrong.

One day Arleta, who grew up with them and knew the whole story, slipped. She was talking too much—like always—about some old movie she'd seen, where the hero comes home to find the heroine pregnant, and she said, "Just like you and Roger, Carole!" She didn't know I was in the room. After that, I started asking questions.

I finally got Arleta to tell me the name of the music student—my real father. I went to meet him at a restaurant and he told me he already had a family and his wife knew nothing about me. He also said that I must never try to contact him again, or I'd be in big trouble.

When you're 13, that kind of threat carries a lot of weight, so I never did. All I knew was that in one short period of time, I'd lost any chance of a real father.

It was then I decided never to have children. I simply didn't want to get involved in all the emotional entanglements that seem to come with having them. I put all my efforts into music, and several years later, when your father and I were married, we agreed that my music career and his law career were all we had room for in our lives.

When you came along, Nicole, I have to admit it was a shock. We loved you, yes, but we agreed that we both had to hold on to our goals. But that wasn't easy with a young child in the house.

As you know, our marriage has not been one of the best. But I still love your father, and when he saw his goal of becoming a judge slipping out of his grasp this summer, he did the only thing he could to hang on to it—he scheduled your abortion. I agreed with him at first that abortion was the best option, but I began having doubts when I saw you struggling.

But your father insisted this was the only solution, and I found myself caught between the two of you. I chose David. I felt I had to. But in thinking it over these past months, I'm not so sure now that I made the best choice.

Nikki stopped reading for a minute, because her head was spinning too much to go on. The whole letter was exactly like her mother was in person—cold, logical, as though she was holding on to her feelings for dear life. It was just like her to draw into herself, to get angry at whoever had hurt her, and stay that way forever.

And then Nikki realized, with a sudden flash of understanding, that she was doing exactly the same thing. And she didn't know how to stop.

There was just a little bit more of the letter, about how Mrs. Sheridan had made everybody in the family promise not to tell

Nikki. She wanted to do it herself. And that no matter how she tried, she could never quite bring herself to, because it was too painful. And Nikki couldn't help noticing that even after everything that had happened between them, her mother never used the words *I'm sorry*. Or, *I was wrong*.

She sat for a few minutes, staring into the air in front of her, trying to take it all in, then she got up and went down the hall to Marta's room and knocked softly.

"Come in," Marta called, and her voice sounded tense and strained. Nikki opened the door and looked inside, and then she saw why. With one arm, Marta was pushing down the top of her suitcase with all her might, and with the other hand, she was trying to force the zipper closed around it. Any other time, Nikki would have laughed and rushed to help her. But not tonight.

She held out the letter to her aunt. Marta took one look at her face, then stood up straight and reached for the paper immediately. Behind her, the top of the suitcase flew open, and hastily-packed clothes spilled over the edges.

Marta scanned her sister's letter quickly, then handed it back and said only, "Come on with me, Nik." She walked to her parents' room, where a thin line of light showed under the door. She knocked and explained what had just happened, and in a few seconds, Nikki's grandparents came to the door in their robes. The four of them made their way downstairs to the kitchen table.

Nikki spread the letter on the table for her grandparents to read. Then she sat silently, waiting.

When they finished reading, they looked at each other, and Grandpa shook his head slowly. "We thought we were doing the right thing not to tell her. We thought if we just gave her enough love and security, it would all work out. But your mother never forgave us. She found out at what was probably the worst possible time for her—she was just 13 and starting to deal with all the things teens have to deal with at that age. She accused us of lying to her, she said she'd never trust us again, and she did everything she could to find her father. But—as you can tell from what you read in the journal—finding him only made things worse. She's never really gotten over it.

"And," he continued, "we worried when we saw that she wasn't telling you, Nikki. She insisted that she had to be the one to do it and made us promise that we wouldn't. But as the years went by, we got more and more concerned. I'm sorry you had to find out this way, honey. I thought she'd at least tell you in person."

Gram nodded her head, agreeing with him.

"What I don't understand," Nikki told Grandpa, "is how you could just . . . go ahead and accept everything that happened—with Gram, I mean. And still go on." She stopped for fear she would hurt Gram by saying more.

"It wasn't the easiest thing I've ever done," Grandpa answered, covering Gram's hand with his own and smiling at her as he spoke. "But everybody gets run over by life sooner or later. It's how you handle it that makes all the difference. You have to let go of the hurt, Nikki, because a life without forgiveness is no life at all. That's what I was trying to tell you the other night in the study."

"But how? How could you just . . . forgive that way?"

"Because Someone once did it for me, Nikki. So you might say I had a kind of road map to follow."

Nikki finally found the courage to say the words she'd been trying to say all along. "I guess this means I'm not even your real granddaughter then, am I?"

She thought she would never forget the look that crossed

Grandpa's face. He got up and knelt beside her chair and put both arms around her. To Nikki, it was the only good part of the whole night.

"Understand this, Nikki," he said. "No one, no one in this whole world, could ever be more my 'real' granddaughter than you are. From the minute I laid eyes on you, I loved you. Not *like* you were my own, but because you *are* my own."

So many thoughts raced through her mind as she looked into her grandfather's face that she could hardly sort them out—that she wasn't the only one who had had tough situations to work through, that she'd been totally ignorant about what had really gone on in her grandparents' lives. And most of all, that some people, like Grandpa, understood what it meant to truly love someone. And that his kind of love was pretty much a mystery to her.

❧ *Fourteen* ❧

NIKKI'S MIND WAS IN A DAZE when she woke Wednesday morning. Her restless sleep had been peopled with Gram as a scared, pregnant teenager, and Grandpa as a heartbroken soldier. And then there was her mother.

Her mother had been in all her dreams—as a lost, frightened teenager, searching for her father, unable to come to terms with what she'd learned about her personal history.

Nikki watched herself in the wavy dresser mirror as she brushed her hair and put in the coral-colored, star-shaped earrings that matched her turtleneck.

It was all so confusing—that all of this could have happened in her own family and she'd never even known.

And to make it worse, the court date is only nine days away, and I still don't know what to do, Evan. I don't have a home to offer you, she said silently, staring at her reflection but seeing the round, blue-eyed face of her infant son. *Not a stable home, with two grown-up parents who love you. And I won't for a long, long time—way too long for you to wait.*

144

She figured in her mind for a minute. *Even if I got married by the time I was, say, 25, you'd be eight already.* And everybody in psychology class and on TV talk shows was always saying how important those early years were. Even she knew that.

"But I'm not ready to just give you up either," she whispered toward the mirror. "I thought I was, but I was wrong."

She grabbed her purse and ran downstairs. It always amazed her how much easier it was to control her crying when she was around other people.

When Keesha was in school, she kept Nikki up to date on all the hall talk—who broke up with whom, who got caught drinking or doing drugs in the bathrooms.

But even without Keesha's antennae, Nikki picked up the growing buzz about Bryce Putnam.

"Did you hear what Bryce said about Chad?" asked several girls whose lockers bordered Nikki's.

"He says Chad's a liar," a girl named Marisa said.

"And a lousy cheat," a second girl said.

"He says Chad's not going to get away with it either," added another.

That afternoon, Gram and Grandpa brought Gallie home from the vet. They were still getting the dog settled in his basket in the kitchen when Nikki came in from school. She swallowed hard when she saw how he looked, lying there with his hind leg all bandaged, wagging his tail weakly at the sight of her. She crouched by his bed and rubbed his golden ears lovingly.

"I'm sorry, boy," she whispered and leaned her cheek against the top of his silky head. "I'm really, really sorry." She went to the pantry and found the box of dog biscuits and took a handful to where Gallie lay, kneeling beside him again. He laid one of his front paws in her lap, and she stroked it gently. "Grandpa says you'll be able to hop around any day now."

On Thursday, Chad found Nikki in the library, reading Dickens. Nikki had spent so much time on make-up work from when she had the baby that she was late getting started on her English paper. She was working extra to catch up, even going to the library during lunch to do research.

Chad slid into the chair beside her.

"Oh, man, how can you stand to read this junk?" he asked, pulling the book toward him and scanning the small print in disgust.

"If I don't read this 'junk,' what exactly do you suggest I do for references, genius?" she asked, retrieving the volume from him.

"Make something up. I always do. Don't you know by now that teachers never check references, especially if it's something they've never heard of. They just figure they haven't read that book yet, you know? The problem with you—" Chad picked up her hand and intertwined his fingers with her own "—is that you're afraid to live dangerously."

He leaned close and brushed his lips against her cheek and waggled his eyebrows suggestively.

"Well, it sounds to me," she shot back, "as though you're doing just fine in the dangerous living department. It's all over school—what Bryce is saying about you."

Chad blew out his breath in a burst of derision. "Bryce is an idiot, and he's full of hot air. The guy got suckered, and he's steamed about it."

"But you're the one who suckered him!"

"Can I help it that he's stupid?" Chad asked.

"No. But you could make it right. I mean, you did cheat him out of the tickets."

Chad pushed back his chair and stood up, and his dark eyes glittered down at her. "How do you know what really happened? Were you there? How about if you just get off my back about Bryce?" Then he went on as though nothing had happened. "Now listen, we're gonna need to leave right after classes on Friday to get to the concert on time."

"On time?" Nikki asked. "It doesn't start till eight. If we leave at 2:30, we'll be there before six."

"I'm not getting stuck halfway to the back door this time. We're gonna be right up front, where the party is. You know what I mean?"

That same afternoon, Keesha was due home from the hospital with her baby. Nikki and four of Keesha's other friends were waiting in the living room with presents and balloons as she walked in the door, hunched over slightly from the pain of the C-section incision.

"Get out of here!" Keesha laughed weakly. "I can't believe you guys. This is really sweet." She leaned against the wall, obviously weak, and didn't even attempt any jokes, so Nikki reassured her quickly.

"Don't worry, we're not staying. This is just a little mini-shower, kind of a . . . a *drizzle*, okay?"

They helped her to the recliner, then fussed over baby Serena while Keesha opened the five packages. There was loud laughter and talk about returning gifts when two of the packages were found to contain identical sleepers with pink gingham-and-lace collars.

"Don't you worry about returning a single thing," Keesha's

mother said, folding the sleepers and laying them on the table beside Keesha's coat. "Babies go through a lot of these, and this little peanut will never notice if two of them are the same." She looked fondly at Serena, whose dark rosebud mouth was open wide in a yawn. Then she got to her feet. "Well, ladies, it's been a long trip home for my girl—both my girls—so . . ."

The other four were out the door when Keesha called Nikki back. Nikki, who had managed to get through the visit without holding the baby, turned uneasily and walked back to where Keesha sat holding her daughter. "What?" she asked.

"Thanks, Nik, for the shower—I mean the *drizzle*," she laughed. "And for getting me to the hospital and, well, just for everything." She looked down at the baby and her face glowed. "You know, you didn't even get to hold her. Here." She held out the blanket-wrapped infant, and Nikki had no choice but to take the child in her arms.

She stood absolutely still for a minute, staring at tiny Serena. The baby breathed a small, shuddering sigh in her sleep, and her eyes moved behind her delicate, black-fringed lids. Nikki swallowed, then swallowed again. Then she thrust the baby back into Keesha's arms, saying she'd be late getting home if she didn't hurry. She turned and rushed out the door, ignoring Mrs. Riley's good-bye.

Every night now, the dream about Evan returned. Nikki dreaded turning out the light, and she sat up as late as she could, reading, listening to the radio, anything she could think of to hold the dream at bay.

I have to resolve this, she thought. *I have to figure out what I'm going to do on the 12th.* She could still hear Chad's words: "When are you gonna stop letting everybody push you around? Nobody can *make* you give up your baby, you know."

She tried not to think about what it would do to Jim and Marilyn Shiveley if she changed her mind and told them she had to have Evan back.

She pictured Mrs. Riley hovering over Keesha, loving and caring for her daughter and granddaughter, and Nikki wished with a sudden, fierce pang of longing that her own mother would, just once, look at her that way.

Maybe if she had ever loved me at all, I wouldn't be in this mess, Nikki thought, staring at the wall before her. *Maybe if I'd had parents who cared, everything would be different.*

But at the same time, Grandpa's words echoed in her ears. *"When you're so angry at someone, you end up carrying them around in your mind all the time. . . . It's easier in the long run to forgive. . . ."*

She'd brushed those words away when he said them in the study, but she couldn't do that any longer. Not after what she'd learned in her mother's letter.

". . . the two go hand in hand, being forgiven and forgiving."

Nikki shook her head, still amazed at the idea of Gram, pregnant with another man's child. How could Grandpa just let her go completely free?

". . . Someone once did that for me, Nikki. So you might say I had a kind of road map to follow."

She might have known it would have something to do with religion, but try as she might, she couldn't make the words mean anything in her own mind.

It was a lot like talking to Jeff, that night in front of the fire. "I got to the place where I'd messed up so many times, I couldn't stand to look at myself in the mirror," he'd said. It hadn't made any sense then. It only irritated her.

If Jeff thinks he messed up, then I'm farther gone than he could ever dream of. I slept with T.J., I ended up pregnant, I've been furiously mad at my parents for so long. . . . She stopped and considered.

Even that's not the whole truth. I hate my parents.

For just a minute, there was satisfaction in facing the feeling head on. Then, just as quickly, the satisfaction was washed away in a flood of guilt.

No matter what they've done, hating them can't be right. But I can't make myself stop feeling this way. . . .

Nikki sat staring at the wall with no sense of time. *I wish I could be like Grandpa, but I can't. I never will. There's too much anger inside, and I don't have any idea what to do about it.*

Chad's face flashed into her mind. *I'm a lot more like him than I ever will be like Grandpa.* "The only way to work through this is just to let your anger all out," Chad had quoted the therapist, but Nikki thought about his drinking, about the way he drove—always just beyond the limit of what was safe—and about the situations he put himself in at school.

So when you finally let all your anger out, she wondered, *is that the end of it? Or does it just make more?*

In classes the next day, it seemed to Nikki that half the school was going to the Alternative Nation concert. The students' attention to anything academic was at an all-time low, and Mr. Keaton, like many of the other teachers, lost his battle to remain calm several times during class. It was a relief when the final bell rang and Nikki could hurry to the parking lot to meet Chad at his car.

Bright sunshine reflected off the dirty hills of snow that had been pushed to each end of the lot by the snowplows, and everywhere there was the sound of dripping. On the soccer field and side lawn of the school, wide ovals of brown grass had been growing larger all day, showing the effects of the crystal-clear blue sky that seemed to extend forever behind and beyond the warm yellow sun. It was a good thing the weather had changed, too, Nikki thought, because Gram and Grandpa would never have let her go so far to a concert if the roads were still icy. As far as they knew, ice was the only reason for Gallie's accident. With Chad's glib explanations, the word *drinking* had never even come up. And Nikki had made him promise he wouldn't drink at all before they left for Chicago.

The hard-packed mass of snow behind the LaSabre's front tire collapsed to the ground with a spongy sound when Chad opened his door. "Great day for a drive to Chicago, huh?" he said, drumming his usual rhythm on the warm, bare metal of the car roof. "The roads'll be clear all the way down there." He eyed the sky suspiciously. "And back, too, if that lousy lake-effect snow doesn't start up again."

"Did you hear how many people from school are going?" Nikki asked as they turned onto the highway.

"Practically the whole place," Chad laughed. "That's all anybody talked about today. Hey, it'll be worth it. This is the biggest band that's come this close in ages, from what people tell me."

"I heard Bryce was going," Nikki said.

Chad gave her a sideways look and shrugged.

"He's still saying all that stuff about how he's gonna get even with you."

"Dum, dum, da-dum. Dum, da-dum dum dum dum dum." Chad intoned the theme of the familiar funeral procession. "Yeah, I'm shaking, can't you tell? How many times do I have to explain it to you? The guy's full of hot air, Nik. He'll never lay a finger on me. Now would you stop worrying about Bryce—" his voice turned low and theatrical "—the Bogeyman?"

"Keesha came home yesterday," Nikki said to change the subject. "A few of us went over and gave her presents for the baby."

"Nice," Chad said. "How's the kid?"

"She's fine. Really pretty, with these huge dark eyes. You should see her."

"How's Keesha gonna take care of this kid? By herself, I mean."

"Well, she's not going to do it by herself," Nikki explained. "Her whole family's helping. They'll watch the baby while she finishes school, and then she'll get a job and maybe go to college. . . ."

"Great," he muttered. "Some life for a kid, huh? What about when it gets old enough to ask where its father is? What're they gonna do then?"

"How should I know?" Nikki asked. "It was her decision, not mine. Not everybody gets to grow up in a nice, traditional family with two parents that love—" She remembered too late about Chad's parents and broke off, midsentence. "Sorry, Chad."

"Aw, who cares?" he said, staring ahead at the straight, smooth strip of pavement ahead of them. "You can start out with two decent parents and still end up in a weird situation. I'm not going anywhere *near* marriage, I can tell you that."

"That's pretty drastic, isn't it?"

"Why should I? Do you know anybody who expects to stay married these days? I sure don't. And look what happens to the kids when you break it up—it just hurts everybody involved."

His voice turned suddenly fierce. "Except maybe the one who does the leaving. I guess if you're the one who walks away, you must have something pretty good to go to. Then *you* get to be the one who calls your kids and tells them how much you miss them, and how you can't wait to see them again—even though you never make any effort to actually *do* that, of course. Words are so easy."

He shook his head slowly, mimicking a woman's high voice, "'Take care of yourself, Chad. Be careful driving that car of yours, honey, because I love you.'"

"Everybody keeps telling me," Nikki began, hesitant because it was as near as she'd ever come to confiding in Chad about things that really mattered, "that you have to let go of it eventually. That when people hurt you, you have to forgive—"

"And just let 'em off the hook, right? Let 'em go scot-free? Well, I don't buy that. I say you don't let anybody hurt you like that. You get even, that's what you do. Somebody hurts me, I'm gonna hurt them right back."

"Is that why you drink?" Nikki asked, surprising herself. She tried to make it sound a little better. "Because you want to hurt your mother back?"

Chad stared straight ahead at the road for a few seconds, then reached over and punched the power button on the radio. The wail of country music filled the car, then elevator music, then rock, as he searched the dial. He forced a smile in Nikki's direction. "Hey, it's party time, right? No more talk about Bryce, or my old lady, or any other kind of gloom and doom, okay?"

The early evening air was cooling rapidly by the time they parked the car. Chad grabbed his black backpack in one hand and Nikki's hand in the other and pulled her along behind him from the parking garage to the arena 10 blocks away.

"I'm not getting stuck a mile from the stage like last time!" he yelled, rushing her down the sidewalk. As they neared the arena, Nikki could see a steady stream of people starting to converge from all directions.

When they were within 15 feet of the glass doors, he looked

back at the rapidly swelling crowd behind.

"Made it!" he said, squeezing Nikki's hand. "It'll be kind of a long wait, but once they open the doors, we can get right up front."

As darkness fell, the wind picked up, and Nikki zipped her down coat snug under under her chin and pulled gloves from her pocket and slipped them over her bluish fingers. After the first half hour of waiting, Nikki was glad for the packed-in crowd around her. The other bodies blocked the wind at least a little, but even so, her fingers were growing numb.

Chad saw the shiver that ran through her and put his arms around her. "You're gonna love it, Nik. This is my absolute favorite band. You should've seen the show they put on in New York."

By the end of an hour, her legs ached dully from the cold. She stood with her forehead bowed against Chad's shoulder, in the circle of his arms that didn't seem to shut out much of the wind. As they waited, he swayed back and forth gently, pulling her with him, and kept up a whispered commentary in her ear on the crowd around them.

"There's a really fat guy right behind you, in jeans that would fit a Mack truck," he said, his lips on her hair as he spoke. "I sure hope you don't get stuck in the mosh pit with *him*—one hit from those hips and you'd be smashed flat."

Nikki shook her head against his shoulder. "You're not very nice about people who have anything wrong with them," she protested.

"Oh, yeah? You should see the girl with him. We're talking terminal acne here. It'd take mountain-climbing equipment just to navigate that face. Don't get close to her in the mosh pit either. I hear ugliness is contagious."

Nikki giggled in spite of herself, even though Chad's casual cruelty shocked her. She glanced up at him. "I don't do mosh pits, anyway, so don't worry."

Chad drew back in mock amazement. "You don't 'do' mosh pits? Whoa, that's one seriously antisocial attitude you've got there, babe. We'll have to see what we can do about that."

Suddenly, the doors swung open, and Chad pulled off his backpack and slipped one of its straps over her arm.

"What . . . why did you—?" she tried to ask, but her voice was drowned in the swell of sound from the crowd around her as they surged inside to the welcome warmth of the arena.

By the time they found a place near the front, Chad was grinning. "This is great," he said, looking up at the stage 10 feet in front of them. "The only problem is, you can't do any serious crowd surfing here." He leaned against the security fence and stretched out his arm toward the stage as far as it would go, then turned back to Nikki. "You're not gonna miss anything tonight. I can tell you that for sure."

"Well, I missed one thing already," she said. "Why am I carrying your backpack?"

Chad touched the tip of her nose with one finger. "Simple. Security people don't check girls like you nearly as close as they do guys like me."

Nikki frowned and slipped the backpack off her shoulder. "What's in here, anyway?" she asked, flipping open the buckle.

Chad grabbed the backpack from her hands. "Let's not get too nosy, okay?"

"What'd you make me carry in here for you?" She stared into his dark eyes that glittered in the reflection from the spots and stage lights, and reached out to take the bag back.

"No way, babe," Chad said and held the pack out of her reach.

"You have booze in there, don't you?"

Chad's dark eyebrows drew together over his eyes, but he didn't answer.

"Well?" she demanded.

"Hey, let's not get all steamed up over a little vodka, okay? You don't have to drink it." His mouth smiled at her, but his dark eyes were cold.

"Vodka? You made me carry vodka in here for you? I could have gotten kicked out. Besides, you *promised*—"

"Nikki," Chad broke in, glancing around uneasily, "would you just be quiet? There're security people crawling all over these concerts." Then he shrugged. "Besides, what are you gonna do about it now? Walk home?"

I wonder what else you've got in that backpack, Nikki thought. She opened her mouth to ask him but was startled to see, just a few people away behind Chad's shoulder, two familiar faces.

He turned and followed her glance. Bryce Putnam and Jen Van Kampen were standing just a few people beyond Chad's shoulder. Jen waggled her fingers in a short wave at Nikki, but Bryce glared at both of them.

"Oh, brother," Nikki said, but Chad only shrugged his shoulders casually, as though Bryce's presence mattered nothing to him.

Then a bass guitar thundered to life on stage behind her. She whirled around, startled by the nearly-deafening noise, as the opening act began.

The next half hour passed quickly, as they watched the local band. It was during the break after their performance, as the stage was being reset for Alternative Nation, that Chad made his way to the back of the arena to the snack bar and returned with cups of Coke for both of them.

Nikki sipped hers and watched as Chad reached into the backpack, scanned the crowd quickly, and pulled out a small bottle. He added a splash of vodka to his cup, then looked at Nikki questioningly.

"No way." She shook her head.

He shrugged and stuck the bottle back down in its place.

"How are we supposed to drive home if you get drunk?" she fumed.

"Keep it down, Nik," he said, looking around again. "You have a phobia about people getting drunk, you know that? An alcophobic—that's what you are." He laughed at his own cleverness, then turned serious again. "All anybody could get from this is a little buzz, so just ease up, all right?"

Nikki watched him angrily, thinking about the accident with Gallie and the long drive back to Michigan. Every now and then, a sweet smell she could identify as pot drifted through the air, and two couples on her left, wearing wristbands that showed they'd been carded and were legal age, drank beer after beer.

The crowd grew louder and louder as they waited, and someone cried "Nation!" and soon, like a ripple throughout the arena, people began calling the band's name in unison. "Na-tion, Na-tion, Na-tion, Na-tion!"

The ripple turned into a swell, and everyone began chanting it. "NA-TION, NA-TION, NA-TION, NA-TION!"

Suddenly, the lights went black, and the noise stopped dead. For perhaps five seconds, they stood in near darkness, only the green "Exit" signs glowing on the walls around the perimeter of the arena.

Then, with a loud *whoosh!* a tower of flames ignited in the middle of the black stage. At the same time, dazzling spots burst on and swept the stage, back and forth, their long columns of light crossing and recrossing each other, converging at last on the lead singer, who strode to the very edge of the stage, one fist held high above his head.

Screams erupted from all over the arena, then the music exploded with a deafening roar, filling the air with the throb of bass guitar and drums.

The singer pulled the microphone against his lips and began to belt out the words. Nikki watched as thousands of hands reached into the air, and thousands of bodies moved to the driving pulse of the music. Light boards all across the back of the set flashed red and blue, in perfect tempo with the beat.

At first, Nikki was so caught up in the music that she saw only what was happening on stage, directly in front of her. The lead singer strutted back and forth across the stage, stepping high, screaming lyrics at the crowd, and alternately jabbing his finger at them and using his hand to accentuate the rhythm of his songs. Soon his long, black hair was soaked with sweat, and beads of it dripped onto the shoulders of his black leather vest and down the bulging muscles of his bare arms.

The bass guitarist bent over the frets, his hair a white-blond, close-cropped fringe. Under his sleeveless T-shirt, Nikki could see the taut muscles of his abdomen ripple with each frenetic twist and jump.

She watched as he and the lead singer sang sections of one song back and forth at each other, moving closer and closer across the stage until they finally stood, face to face, their foreheads pressed together above one microphone, shouting the final words in unison. The crowd went wild, and Nikki glanced at Chad.

He was just slipping the vodka bottle back into his black backpack for a second time. He took a long swallow of his spiked Coke and grinned at her, holding up his cup in salute.

Behind him, Nikki saw with surprise that Jen—the same quiet Jen who could never project past row five of the auditorium—was sitting astride Bryce's wide shoulders, both her hands high in the air, screaming out the lyrics with Alternative Nation.

After the first four numbers, there was a startling lull in the noise. All the lights in the arena went out again, and the keyboard player slipped into a plaintive bridge to the next number.

Nikki watched as one small, glimmering light punctured the velvet blackness in which the audience stood. The light was joined in an instant by another, and another, and then hundreds and thousands of soft flames flickered alive throughout the arena as people held pocket lighters aloft, waving them slowly back and forth in time to the music.

In the soft yellow glow of the waving lighters, the faces around her looked wistful, and Nikki found herself caught up in the beauty of the moment.

Chad wrapped his arms around Nikki from behind and rested his chin lightly on the top of her head. They swayed back and forth, back and forth, close and warm in the gently-lit darkness. In the circle of his arms, Nikki found herself wondering where this relationship with Chad was headed. There were so many things about him that bothered her—his drinking, his lying, those kinds of things.

On the other hand, she thought, *when he wants to, he can be just about the most charming guy I've ever met.*

So when Chad tightened his arms around her and started kissing the top of her head, then the back of her neck, she was slower to object than she would normally have been.

But when he whispered in her ear what he thought they should do on the way home, Nikki pushed his arms away.

"*Stop it,* Chad," she whispered, trying to keep her voice low enough so that no one around them would hear.

Chad showed no concern at all about volume. "You know what, Nik?" he asked over the music. "I think you ought to stop pretending to be something you're not."

She swung around to stare at him, and in the glow of the lighters, she could see the side of his mouth turned up in a smirk.

"I don't sleep around!"

Chad gave a short laugh. "Hey, it's not like it'd be the first time. We all know that for sure. Why do you think I take you out, anyway?"

Nikki closed her eyes hard against the quick tears that formed there and turned her back to Chad again. She stood silently, the only still body in the vast, swaying crowd, and behind her she heard Chad pull the vodka bottle from his backpack for at least the third time.

She couldn't think any thoughts that made sense right then, suffocating as she was in waves of anger and shame. But she would think later, looking back, that this quiet, plaintive number was the last sane moment of the concert. As soon as it was over, the band and the crowd erupted into a frenzy that made the opening of the concert, wild as it had been, look calm.

As the guitars and keyboard vamped before the next number, lighters snapped off and glittering spotlights in geometric shapes roamed and flashed across the crowd. People started dancing in place again, their arms high in the air.

The band played the same few chords over and over again, never resolving them, and still the lead singer didn't appear. The guitarist and drummer watched the crowd and laughed, turning up the speed and the volume, so that the fans danced faster and faster, whipped into a kind of uproar that soon reached fever pitch.

At the peak of excitement, the four dazzling stage spots suddenly locked on to a ramp high above the stage. In the center of the ramp stood the lead singer.

The long-tailed jacket he had pulled on over his vest was made of a material that glistened and shimmered in the lights, and when he held his hands over his head and began to clap, the entire audience once again erupted in screams and imitated the rhythm of his clapping.

Even through the red haze of her shattered feelings about Chad, Nikki recognized the song he had looked forward to hearing, "Burn the World." The singer shouted the first phrase, then held the mike toward the crowd to pick up the phrase they shouted back at him. He shouted again; they echoed back.

After the first verse, the singer picked up the tempo until the whole arena seemed submerged in the pulsating beat. People began to push past Nikki to get to the mosh pit, where 20 or more fans were already slam dancing, hurling themselves wildly against each other.

Then Nikki saw Jen, still at shoulder height, being passed over the heads of the crowd. Some of the fans doing the passing were laughing and holding up their arms before Jen got anywhere near them. Others staggered a little on their feet and seemed surprised when people near them yelled, "Get her! Don't drop her!"

Soon other people were spread out above the crowd, "surfing" on the hands stretched out to them. Then, with a little help from some of the bigger fans, an entire section of the security fencing went down. Would-be surfers swarmed across the flat fence and took turns scrambling onto the stage.

"So maybe this'll turn out better than I thought," Chad said, more to himself than to Nikki. Without even trying to hide what he was doing, he reached for the bottle in his backpack, uncapped it, and took another shot. Then he joined the dense crush of people struggling for a place on the stage.

Security officers hurried to get to the broken section of fencing, struggling to push and shove their way through the crowd, but at every turn they found their paths blocked by the sheer numbers of bodies. Meanwhile, crowd surfing off the stage was in full swing.

Nikki stood stock-still, with Chad's "Why do you think I take you out, anyway?" ringing in her head, but she couldn't keep from watching. Chad was easy to follow, tall as he was, with his blond hair that reflected the dazzling lights crisscrossing the crowd. He elbowed his way past the people in front of him, put his hands on the edge of the stage and swung himself up.

He only pretended to be interested in me all this time, Nikki thought as she stared at the back of his head. Everything fell into place as she watched him stand up straight and stretch his arms high just as the lead singer had. And, as things usually worked out for Chad, one of the lights swept across him and seemed to linger, just as he raised his hands.

In that instant, she no longer saw his charm or his great looks or his humor. Instead, she saw his selfishness, his lying, his way of making himself look good at other people's expense. *And his anger. He's so angry about what his mother did that he's all twisted inside.*

She thought of what he'd said about her, and she felt her own anger flare up against him. And as she watched what happened next, it seemed to her that her own violent feelings were somehow responsible.

With security guards fighting their way toward Chad, yelling, "Stop it! Get down from there!" he paused at the edge of the stage—the same kind of pause he'd made at *The Glass Menagerie* rehearsal, to make sure every eye was on him.

Someone shoved a long-necked bottle toward him. He reached down and grabbed it, then lifted it high with his head tilted far back, and Nikki watched for a long minute as his Adam's apple bobbed up and down. Then he tossed the empty bottle back into the crowd, held his hands high above his head again, and hurled himself off the stage.

But from where Nikki stood, she could see what Chad couldn't—that Bryce had just moved into the key position to catch him. Nikki caught a glimpse of Bryce's face in the reflection of the same light that had highlighted Chad, and she saw the anger there.

And she saw, as she would see over and over again every time she shut her eyes for the next several hours, Chad's body dive in slow motion toward the waiting hands. And among those hands was an empty space, where Bryce stood with his arms at his side.

And then she heard Chad—or felt the vibration through her feet, she was never sure which—hit the floor with a sickening crunch. All around his body, screams erupted, and over the top of all of them, Jen's shrill shriek seemed to split the air.

And Nikki thought to herself in a strange, detached way, *I guess Jen's finally learned how to project.*

❦ *Fifteen* ❧

NIKKI PRESSED HER COLD HANDS gratefully against the hot mug of cider she held. She glanced around the Allens' living room at the green-plaid couches and cherry-wood tables and the stonework fireplace flanked by ceiling-to-floor bookshelves.

Jeff lay sprawled on his side before the fireplace, propped on one elbow, the long fingers of his free hand tracing the rich swirls of the green-and-cream oriental rug beneath him. From time to time, he glanced across the shining oval top of the coffee table at Nikki, as though his eyes were drawn by a magnet, then back down quickly at the rug.

Carly rocked endlessly in a rocker beside the fireplace, her feet on the edge of the seat, arms hugging her knees against her chest. Her head was tilted to one side as she took in everything Nikki had been saying.

Looking exhausted, Carl and Marlene Allen, Jeff's parents, had dropped onto the couch facing the love seat where Nikki sat. After answering Nikki's frantic phone call from the arena and dashing 10 miles through the snowy suburbs to the hospital, the Allens had spent two hours in the waiting room with her before they got a final verdict on Chad's condition.

Nikki held the hot cup close to her face and breathed in the cinnamon-scented steam. She closed her eyes and thought back over the last few hours.

Chad's fall had cost him a severe concussion and a badly broken collarbone. Nikki winced, remembering the grotesque swelling that pushed the entire right side of his face out of shape and then began to turn a sickly reddish-purple. His repeated vomiting inflamed the pain and discomfort of his rigidly braced shoulder, and by the time Nikki had left the hospital with the Allens, his right eye had swollen completely shut.

How guilty she'd felt when she looked at him in the hospital bed, as though her anger at him had made her somehow responsible for his injuries.

There had been calls to Gram and Grandpa, and to Chad's father, explaining over and over again all that had happened, calls making arrangements for Chad's hospital stay, calls about his car left in the parking garage. . . . Nikki had thought it would never end.

And then, suddenly, all the busywork was over and the five of them were sitting quietly in front of the Allens' fireplace, sipping hot spiced cider as though it were the most natural thing in the world at 1:30 in the morning.

This was the way Nikki had spent so many afternoons last autumn, on weekend visits, when Carl and Marlene had pored with her for hours over files from the adoption agency as she tried to choose a family for her baby.

And now, here she sat again, struggling to answer Marlene's seemingly casual question about how everything was, now that the pregnancy was behind her.

"Well," Nikki stalled, carefully keeping her voice steady, "okay until tonight. Busy, you know, with school and helping Gram and all that. But okay."

"I'm glad to hear that," Dr. Allen said, "because for some girls, giving up a baby can be one of the hardest things they ever do."

Nikki stared at him and felt her eyes begin to fill. *It's not just me, then?*

She blinked rapidly and tried hard to hold her feelings inside, but it was no use. To her embarrassment, she started to cry in front of them all. Not quiet, neat tears that left her looking charmingly distressed, but huge sobs that welled up from somewhere deep in her middle. All the pain about Evan, all the anger and hurt about her parents, her confusion over what her mother had revealed in her letter, even the secret mortification of Chad's words at the concert—it all poured out of her in what felt like an endless stream of tears as she sat on the love seat with her face in her hands. Marlene moved to her side and put both arms around her as she cried.

Much later, when Nikki finally reached the hiccup-and-sniffle stage, she tried to explain how she felt about giving up the baby.

"I miss him so much, I can't even put it into words. And that feeling got all mixed up with how I felt about my parents and being pregnant and . . . just everything." She blew her nose again and wiped mascara off the back of her hand before she went on. "I thought at first that the answer might be to get the baby back. I mean, I haven't signed the final papers yet, not till next week."

Dr. Allen sat with his hands folded between his knees, listening intently. "And now?" he asked. "Do you still think that's what you need to do?"

"Well, after I saw what Chad did tonight," Nikki said, "I did a lot of thinking at the hospital. Chad's so angry about his mother, about his whole life, that he just keeps making crazy decisions."

Nikki shook her head, trying to clear away the picture of Chad falling through the air. "I don't want to be like that, making bad decisions—I mean, because I'm too angry or in too much pain to think straight. And I guess I've known all along that getting Evan back wouldn't really solve the problem. It would just make me feel better for a little while. I still think a baby needs a stable home and grown-up parents—things I can't give him. I just have to figure out . . . how . . . to let him go."

By this time, Carly was perched on the edge of the coffee table in front of the love seat, almost bouncing with what she wanted to say. "We have friends," Carly was saying, "—well, they're actually friends of Mom and Dad's—who've been trying to have a baby for years and years, and they just adopted the most adorable little girl. You should see her, Nik. She's got these huge black eyes and long curly lashes and—" Carly circled her own head with one extended finger "—these little black ringlets all over her head and—"

"Try to get to the point sometime tonight, Carly," Dr. Allen murmured gently, grinning at his daughter as she spoke.

Carly rolled her eyes at his interruption. "Well, anyway, just last month, they had the most beautiful adoption ceremony at our church, and we were invited, and a bunch of other people who are friends with them, and their family, and they had candles and cake and punch, and they gave each other presents and read all this stuff about adoption from the Bible. And the birth mother wrote a poem and read it and—" Carly threw her hands out to either side exuberantly "—well, I was thinking *you* could do that, Nikki. Have a ceremony, you know? To kind of help you get through this?"

"It was very special." Marlene smiled her slow, warm smile that always reminded Nikki so much of Jeff. "The birth mother told me after it was over that planning and organizing this ceremony really helped her get through the whole process of placing her baby."

"I talked to the caseworker," Dr. Allen said, "and she said that a lot of the birth mothers they see seem to need more than just papers signed in front of a judge to help them finalize the adoption. They need something for their hearts and their spirits, because placing your baby for adoption is far more than just legal paperwork. So somebody—I don't know who—came up with this idea of an adoption ceremony."

"What else do they do? At these ceremonies?" Nikki asked, wadding up her used tissues into a tight ball between her hands.

Marlene joined in. "Each birth mother plans it out the way she wants, with input from her caseworker and the adoptive parents, so every ceremony is different. But at the one we went to, the pastor was there, and family and friends. And the birth mother read some things she'd written, and so did the adoptive parents. The pastor talked about adoption and explained what it means from the Bible."

"Do you like that idea, Nik?" Carly asked.

"I guess so," Nikki answered. "I'm just not big on doing things in front of a lot of people, you know?"

"You'd be the one to decide how many people would be there," Marlene answered. "You could just have your grandparents and Marta and the Shiveleys. And us, too, I hope."

Nikki nodded. "Well, if I ever did it, you guys would have to be there. I couldn't have gotten through this whole thing without you."

Dr. Allen tilted his cup high and drained the last of his cider. "Why don't we sit down tomorrow, after you get back from seeing Chad, and talk about this some more? It certainly shouldn't be a spur-of-the-moment decision. If you decide you want to, you'd have to call the Shiveleys and make sure it's all right with them, too. I have to say, though, I think it could be a big help to you. When we went to the ceremony last month, we all thought of you right away, Nikki."

He glanced at his watch. "But right now, I move we get to bed, because I have rounds to make at the hospital in just about five hours, and what I say to my patients makes a lot more sense when I've had some sleep."

Long after the others had gone upstairs, Nikki sat staring into the embers of the fire that still glowed bright-orange behind the closed glass doors.

She knew she couldn't sleep yet. She wondered about the idea of a ceremony and tried to envision it. Somehow it seemed more appropriate to mark something as big as handing your baby over to another family with a ceremony than with the simple good-byes she had said to Evan at the hospital. And for the first time, she dared to admit to herself that her idea of taking Evan back would fill only her needs, not his. If she was really honest, she couldn't imagine trying to raise him by herself.

Nikki sighed and set her mug down on a coaster. There was a whole lot more to her tears and the pain inside than just losing Evan, though. She had to figure out what it was.

It seems as though every hurt inside me turns to anger, to hate. My parents were wrong, I know they were—to try to make me kill the baby when I was pregnant. But how I feel about them is just as wrong.

And tonight, when Chad said what he did at the concert, I was so angry at him that I wanted to hurt him back. Nikki ran her thumb around and around the rim of her empty mug with a hollow, squeaking sound. *Grandpa says you never regret the times you forgave, only the times you didn't, and that's fine for him.* She thought about what Grandpa had done—marrying Gram when she was pregnant with somebody else's child—and shook her head in amazement.

That's fine for him, but I don't know how to forgive that way. It's like that part of me doesn't even work.

"It wouldn't be the first time. We all know that for sure." Chad's words were like the stab of a sword. *It was mean, sure, but it was true. And everyone in school who saw me pregnant knows it, so why did it make me so furious?*

Nikki sat without moving a muscle, trying to look inside herself and understand what was going on. Suddenly, a thought began to take shape in her mind.

I'm angry because what Chad said is true—because I did get pregnant, because I did something I knew was wrong. And I hate myself for it.

It was a new thought to her, a feeling she realized she'd been wrestling with for a long time. But she'd never been able to put it into words before.

I don't know how to forgive myself for what I did. Any more than I can forgive my parents or Chad.

Nikki looked even further back, into the spring of the previous year and the date with T.J.—the night she'd gotten pregnant. *And T.J.,* she thought. *How could I ever forgive him?*

She was so lost in her thoughts that she jumped, startled, when Jeff sat down beside her. When he spoke, his voice was soft.

"Nik, can I help?"

She turned and stared at his familiar face, at the fuzzy dark hair growing back in all over his head, and the concern in his eyes stirred memories of their conversation the week before.

"I think I'm in really big trouble," she said, her lips trembling. "And I don't just mean because of . . . because of the baby."

Jeff nodded, his eyes intent on hers as he listened carefully.

"It's everything, Jeff. I'm so angry inside, I can't even explain it. At first, when I found out I was pregnant, I just tried to block it out of my mind. And when my parents tried to make me have the abortion, I tried to pretend it wasn't happening. And when the baby was born and I gave him up for adoption, I thought that would be the end of it.

"But it was just starting. All the pain and the nightmares and the missing him. I couldn't pretend anymore, Jeff. I got really, really angry, at everything and everybody. Most of all, at myself. And the anger is eating me alive inside, and I don't know what to do about it.

"You said last week that you didn't think I could go much further without forgiving my parents, but what if the person you can't forgive most of all is yourself?"

Jeff hesitated for a minute before he answered, lacing his fingers together and pushing, palms out, to crack his knuckles the way he always did when he was trying to think. "Well, God's the one who forgives us and teaches us how to forgive other people. But if the connection between you and God is broken—" he shrugged, then had an idea. "Wait a minute. You know that conference I told you about, back at Christmastime? They showed us something there that might help."

He pulled open the door of the end table and took out a pencil and scratch pad from the Scrabble game stowed inside. He riffled through the pages of the little tablet until he found one that was blank, then drew a horizontal line on the right and one on the left.

"Okay, pretend these two things are cliffs, all right? This side is where we are—" he wrote the word *us* on the cliff on the left "— and this is where God is." He penciled in the word *God* on the cliff on the right.

Then he pointed to the empty space between. "You see this big hole?"

Nikki nodded.

"The verse they taught us at the conference was Isaiah 59:2, where it says, 'Your iniquities have separated you from your God.' So the problem is what to do about our sins, because that's what makes this big gap we can never cross. Sometimes people think if they could just be really good from now on, then they'd be all right. But the Bible says we can't get to God by doing good things. And besides, that wouldn't take care of all the wrong stuff we've already done, right?"

"I guess not," Nikki answered.

Jeff wrote the word *holy* under the word *God*. "And to make it even worse, God is holy, so He punishes sin. But along with being holy, He also loves us. Just like you love your baby, that's how God loves you, Nikki."

Nikki stared at the scrap of paper in front of her. That big hole in the middle—she could understand that. It felt as though a world of wind could sweep through the chasm between her and God.

"So He sent Jesus, who 'bore our sins in His body on the tree.'" Jeff drew a horizontal line connecting the two cliffs, then slashed a vertical line through it to form a cross. "Jesus took the punishment we should get, when He was on the cross, because He loves us so much that He wants to adopt us into His family. So He's the bridge between us and God, see? And if we believe that, and receive Him as our Savior and Master, we can cross over to this side."

Jeff turned toward her on the love seat. "So, does that make any sense to you, Nik?"

Nikki bit at the skin of her bottom lip, still staring at the little paper on Jeff's lap. That hole, that huge, empty cavern between her and God—*that's exactly how it feels*, she thought. *Exactly. Like there's no one there when I try to talk to Him. Not that He'd listen to me, anyway. Not after everything I've done.*

The words Jeff had said—"Just like you love your baby, that's how God loves you, Nikki"—played over and over in her mind, but she couldn't grasp their meaning any more than she could understand the long conversations at the end of her Spanish book, the ones with vocabulary words she hadn't studied yet.

"Does it?" Jeff repeated.

"Does it make sense to me?" She echoed his question awkwardly, drawing her legs up underneath her on the couch. "I just think too much has happened tonight, you know? It's kind of hard to concentrate."

Jeff watched her closely, then put down his pencil. "Yeah, I can understand that." He stretched out his long, jeans-clad legs in front of him and propped his feet against the coffee table.

Nikki glanced sideways at his profile in the orange glow of the fireplace and thought how crazy she'd been to be irritated by Jeff's attempts to help her over the past week or so. How different he was from Chad!

Nikki cleared her throat, then spoke hesitantly. "You know, you were right about Chad. Last weekend, I mean. I should've listened to you."

Jeff turned his hands over, palms up, in his "oh well" gesture.

"No, really," she said. "I just . . . I was awfully rude to you."

"Nik, you already said you were sorry, remember? At the hospital?"

"I know. But I wanted to explain why. Every time I saw you, it reminded me of last summer, when I first found out I was pregnant. Of deciding to give the baby up for adoption. And I kind of wanted to . . . to push you away so I wouldn't remember, you know?"

Jeff turned his head and grinned at her. "Yeah, but I was too dumb to see it and back off. I was stupid to get so pushy about you going out with Chad. . . ."

"No, you were right—" she tried to put in, but Jeff shook his head.

"It wasn't my place to tell you what to do." He slid his feet to the floor and sat forward, hands between his knees. "Since we're doing true confessions and all, I guess I have one, too. I suppose it's no secret—Carly tells me the whole world knows from the way I've been acting—but I think I've cared about you, without knowing it, for a long time, Nik."

Nikki stared down at her lap, surprised at the warm feeling that seemed to grow inside her as he spoke.

"It took what happened last summer, when you were in such a mess, to make me finally figure out how I felt." He gave a short laugh. "Brilliant, huh? Well, anyway, that's why I acted like I did, trying to make sure you were safe and all that kind of stuff."

Nikki opened her mouth to reassure him, but Jeff went on speaking. "But I can see you've got too much going on right now—too many things to work through. And I sure don't want to get in your way. So you'll be glad to know, Nik, that after last weekend, I decided I'm gonna just kind of get on with my own life and quit bugging you."

One glance in her direction then would have shown Jeff the effect his words had on her, the sadness in her eyes, but he only stared straight ahead into the fire. "I guess I'm kind of slow, you know? But you can quit worrying, Nikki. I think I finally got the point."

He turned and ripped the picture he'd drawn off the little scratch pad and held it out to her. "Anyway, take this, okay? In case you want to give it some more thought someday."

She took it, silently.

"And, Nik? I hope we'll always stay friends. You know, keep in touch and stuff. What d'you think?"

Nikki hugged her arms tighter around her chest and looked away from his eyes into the gray-white ashes of the fireplace. "Oh. Definitely."

❧ *Sixteen* ❧

NIKKI CROSSED ONE LEG OVER the other and jiggled her foot impatiently. She tugged at the waistband of her skirt, trying to ease the way the belt cut into her middle as she sat in the front pew of the small stone chapel. *I hope this is the right thing to do.* She had turned the idea of an adoption ceremony over and over in her mind and finally decided that this was what she wanted.

The rubbery *thud* of a tennis ball being batted back and forth drifted in through the open windows of the chapel from the nearby college tennis courts, along with the sweet, green scent of fresh-mown grass. Then came the triumphant shout, far away but perfectly distinct: "Six-love! Hah! Skunked you!"

It's hard to believe Chad and I were standing in line, freezing, at the concert just a week ago today. It's like spring came overnight this year, Nikki thought, glancing out the open windows framed by leaded-glass, diamond-shaped panes on either side of the nave.

At least, outside it did. Inside her, the huge emptiness seemed to keep growing.

Earlier, as they were driving from Rosendale to the chapel at

Howellsville College, Arleta kept shaking her head and saying from the backseat of Nikki's grandparents' car, "NEVER SAW SPRING COME THIS EARLY IN MARCH IN MY ENTIRE LIFE. MARK MY WORDS, WE HAVE MORE SNOW COMING. 'IN LIKE A LAMB, OUT LIKE A LION,' REMEMBER THAT? THE FARMER'S ALMANAC SAID A LATE SPRING THIS YEAR, AND I'VE NEVER KNOWN IT TO BE WRONG."

Nikki glanced to her right, where, from her place on the pew on the other side of Gram, Arleta was still going on about the weather in her imitation of a whisper. *Which just means,* Nikki thought, *that you can hear everything she says only halfway through the church instead of all the way.*

"I JUST CAN'T GET OVER IT. HAVE YOU EVER SEEN IT WARM LIKE THIS AT THE BEGINNING OF MARCH, CAROLE?"

Gram shook her head in answer and patted Arleta's arm to quiet her. To her left, Nikki saw Grandpa's lips tighten as he tried to hold in a grin.

"Can't take that woman anywhere," he whispered to Nikki from the side of his mouth.

It had been Grandpa's idea to hold the adoption ceremony at Howellsville College, where he'd taught biology for years and years. Nikki had been uncomfortable with the big, echoing sanctuary of the Rosendale church, where a dozen people would rattle around looking lost, but she'd wanted some place more formal than her grandparents' house.

She glanced around the tiny chapel, at the walnut wood of the pulpit, pews, and window frames that warmed the gray stone interior, and smiled at the Allens in the seat behind her.

She wondered for a moment how it would feel to have her own parents there, sitting on either side of her, supporting her. As though she could read Nikki's thoughts, Gram reached over and covered Nikki's right hand with her own. Grandpa watched, and then reached for her left hand, giving it a reassuring squeeze. Marta, on the other side of her father, pushed her glasses back into place and gave her niece an encouraging smile.

Nikki felt a lump swell in her throat, and she swallowed hard. *Can I really do this? Can I hold Evan again, see him again, without crying? And then give him away for good?*

Even though the papers she would sign later that day before the judge specified an open adoption, which meant she could see the baby frequently, Nikki knew things would never be the same after that day. For just a second, she squeezed her grandparents' hands tight, holding on. Then Marilyn and Jim Shiveley walked in.

Just as they'd rehearsed the night before, Marilyn and Jim brought the baby to Nikki, and as Marilyn handed the baby carefully to her, Nikki glanced up, then caught her breath at what she saw in the older woman's face.

Love for the baby stood unmasked in Marilyn's eyes, love that matched Nikki's own, and it made her look fragile and vulnerable somehow. As she looked, Nikki knew that handing the baby back even for these short moments had cost Marilyn something.

Jim set a bulging diaper bag on the red carpet beside Nikki's feet, then crouched beside it. He pulled open a zipper and pointed to two bottles nestled there.

"Here's formula, Nikki, in case he cries," Jim whispered. "But he may not take it. This time of day, he usually prefers juice, so here's apple juice in the clown bottle. And—" Jim dug lower into the diaper bag and pulled out a brightly-colored bit of rubber and plastic "—here's his pacifier and—"

Marilyn rubbed her hand gently over her husband's shoulder and smiled. "I think she can handle it, honey. C'mon."

Jim grinned at Nikki in apology. "Sorry, Nikki." He got to his feet, but his eyes seemed unwilling to leave the baby's face. He reached down and pulled the satin-rimmed corner of the teddy-bear blanket, which had fallen over Evan's cheek, back into place. Then the Shiveleys took their seats in the front pew on the other side of the aisle.

Gram and Grandpa's pastor stepped to the front of the small group and opened his Bible.

"Please listen as I read these words from the one hundred and thirty-ninth psalm," he said. "'O Lord, you have searched me and you know me. . . .'"

Nikki snuggled Evan's warm weight close to her, luxuriating in the feel and the smell and the sight of him against her chest. His perfectly puckered red lips parted a little each time he breathed, each breath a slight feathery sound that shook his lower lip. Nikki watched, fascinated at how he responded to any noise or sudden movement with a quick sucking motion, his tongue pressing rapidly against the roof of his mouth for a few seconds until he was comforted.

"'For you created my inmost being; you knit me together in my mother's womb,'" the pastor's voice read on. "'I praise you because I am fearfully and wonderfully made; your works are wonderful, I know that full well.'"

Nikki thought back to the first time she'd seen Evan, on the ultrasound at the clinic—how he'd flown into a flurry of movement when she sneezed during the procedure. It was then she'd known that she had no right to take this tiny person's life from him.

Tears spilled over onto her cheeks as she watched his long-lashed eyes flutter delicately, thinking how close she'd come to doing just that.

I can't keep you, Evan, sweet, sweet baby, but just knowing you're in the world somewhere, drinking bottles and being this beautiful, will keep me going. She ducked her head and kissed his soft forehead.

"Nicole, would you and Marilyn and Jim come up, please?" the pastor said.

They took their places side by side in front of the intricately-carved walnut table where a wreath of candles waited. The pastor struck a match, then spoke as he held the flame to the tip of the first candle.

"This candle represents Nicole Sheridan, Evan's birth mother, who with great courage allowed her son to be born into a world where so many babies are now denied that right. And then to be adopted into the loving arms of a family, where he will be cherished and protected and nurtured.

"This candle—" he touched the flame of the first candle briefly to the top of another "—is for Evan, whose life we celebrate, and whose future we recognize as being planned by God, just as we read in verse 16 of Psalm 139.

"And this candle," he said as he lit a third, "is for the Shiveleys, who have opened their hearts and their home to Evan and have committed themselves to mother him and father him, to be his family forever."

Nikki gazed down at the baby, and her arms tightened around him. The weight of love she felt was staggering, and for a second, she wondered that she could stand underneath it.

"This, then, is the true meaning of adoption in Ephesians chapter one." The pastor's voice startled Nikki back into the present, and she looked up to listen. "It's an idea that originated with God, the perfect father. That a couple, such as Jim and Marilyn Shiveley, would choose to love a child as God chose to love us, would choose to share completely all that is theirs—material, emotional, and spiritual—with that child, as God has chosen to do with us."

Nikki could hear again the words Jeff had spoken the week before, when she sat with him in the living room of his family's house in Chicago. *"Just like you love your baby, that's how God loves you, Nikki."*

All week long, those words had echoed in her mind, but they had been just beyond the grasp of her understanding. Until now.

Standing there in front of the chapel, holding Evan, feeling her love for him, she wondered, *Could it really be true? Could God really feel that way about me?*

"And," the pastor went on, looking at Nikki, "that a mother would love her child so much and so wisely that she would choose what is best for him, at such great cost to herself. As God chose what was best for us, even though it meant giving up His own Son, Jesus Christ, to die a terrible death on the cross, where He carried our sin and our punishment so that we could be forgiven."

"Carried our sin," her mind repeated. *"So that we could be forgiven."*

For weeks, the enormity of her feelings for the baby had towered over everything she did, everything she thought. But now Nikki felt as though she stood in the presence of a love far greater than her own, a love that dwarfed her own emotions.

She looked down again at the baby, but his sleeping face blurred in her vision. And this time the tears were from far more than just her feelings about Evan.

The Shiveleys stepped together to the microphone. The ceremony was going on, and Nikki looked around the room, amazed that no one seemed to see what was happening inside her. She rocked Evan back and forth slightly, instinctively, and tried to contain the thought that was unfolding, expanding like a sweet melody in her mind. *God loves me. God loves me. Jesus carried our sin—my sin—my anger, my hate. I can be forgiven, adopted.*

Please, God, please forgive me. Thank you for loving me this way.
God loves me.

The moment came for Nikki to place the baby in Marilyn's arms—the moment she had dreaded for weeks. Her arms seemed locked around his small, slumbering form, and her eyes drank in the sight of him there.

It was only the song inside her that gave Nikki strength to tear her eyes away. *God loves me. God loves me.*

She lifted her head and took a step that closed the space between her and the Shiveleys.

Marilyn, her voice just this side of trembling, leaned into the microphone and began to read from the sheet of paper she held in front of her. At first she paused between the lines, glancing from the paper to the baby and back again, then she forgot her audience and began to quote the poem from memory, gazing at Evan as she spoke.

> I
> Did not plant you,
> True,
> But when
> The season is done—
> When the alternate
> Prayers for sun
> And for rain
> Are counted—
> When the pain
> of weeding
> And the pride
> of watching
> Are through—

Then
I will hold you
High
A shining sheaf
Above the thousand
Seeds grown wild.

Not my planting,
But by heaven
My harvest—
My own child.

When Marilyn finished, there was stillness for a moment, then Nikki bent her head and kissed Evan's cheek.

Then softly, almost silently, so that only she and the baby would ever hear, she whispered, "Good-bye, Evan."

She lifted the baby and placed him in Marilyn's arms.

Then Nikki turned to where Gram sat, holding a rosewood box that contained the best of her letters to her infant son. Nikki had spent hours this past week on the window seat in her bedroom, copying and recopying them onto creamy stationery.

Now she took the box from Gram, along with the brightly-wrapped teddy bear she had bought the day before, and held them out to Jim.

"For Evan," she said.

He smiled and put his arms around her, then reached out and drew Marilyn and the baby into their hug, and Nikki listened to their fervent, whispered "thank-yous" and knew her choice had been the right one.

❧ Epilogue ❧

March 13

Dear Jeff,

Thank you for coming to the ceremony yesterday. Sorry I didn't get to talk to you alone, because there're some things I need to tell you.

Remember what you tried to explain to me, that night you came up here and we sat in front of the fire? About how God had kind of "moved in on your heart"? I didn't have a clue what you were talking about then. Or last week when we talked again at your house.

But this past week, I couldn't help remembering one thing you said—that just like I love the baby, God loves me. That didn't make much sense to me either. Not until the ceremony yesterday.

When I stood there holding Evan, it was as though everything fell into place all of a sudden. I really understood, way down deep inside, that God loves me. And it was like I could feel Him right there with me at the ceremony, telling me it was time to accept that love and forgiveness. So I did.

I guess what I really want to say to you is thank you. If you hadn't explained it all to me—even when I was wishing you would leave me alone—I wouldn't have known what was going on. So thanks a lot, Jeff, which doesn't seem like enough after all you've done, but I think you'll understand.

For the first time since the baby was born, I got through the night without the nightmare. What a relief! After I saw Marilyn and Jim with Evan, I stopped worrying about what kind of parents they're going to be.

I'm going to call my mother soon. She wrote me a letter, and I think we're at a place now where maybe we can talk. Keesha said to tell you "hi." She and Serena are both doing fine.

Aunt Marta asked me to go along on one of her trips. She has an interdisciplinary conference (whatever that is) to speak at out in California. Gram and Grandpa think it'll be a great break for me. It'll work out fine with my schedule, 'cuz I'm finally all caught up on schoolwork, except for Spanish, but Marta says there'll be plenty of chances to practice out there, since so many people speak Spanish.

Chad called when he got home from the hospital. He told me you and your dad went to see him, and I thought that was pretty special of you, after everything that's happened. Chad said he told his father about an alcoholism treatment place your dad mentioned, but other than that, it doesn't seem like he's changed much. He's already trying to get tickets for another big concert, in Detroit this time. He even asked if I wanted to go, and I told him there was no way I'd ever go out with him again.

I guess that's all I wanted to say. Thanks again. I hope I'll see you when I get back from California, because I really want to talk to you about everything that's happened.

Nikki